Chinatown

Thuận

CHINATOWN

translated from the Vietnamese
by Nguyễn An Lý

A NEW DIRECTIONS
PAPERBOOK ORIGINAL

Chinatown was first published in Vietnam in 2005 by NXB Đà Nẵng.
This edition is published by arrangement with Tilted Axis.

Manufactured in the United States of America
First published as a New Directions Paperbook Original (NDP1535) in 2022
Design by Erik Rieselbach

Library of Congress Cataloging-in-Publication Data
Names: Thuận, 1967– author. | Nguyễn An Lý, translator.
Title: Chinatown / by Thuận ; translated by Nguyễn An Lý.
Other titles: Chinatown. English
Description: New York : New Directions Publishing Corporation, [2022] |
"A New Directions paperbook original"
Identifiers: LCCN 2021061994 | ISBN 9780811231886 (paperback) |
ISBN 9780811231893 (ebook)
Subjects: LCGFT: Novels.
Classification: LCC PL4378.9.T57493 C4813 2022 |
DDC 895.9/2234—dc23/eng/20220107
LC record available at https://lccn.loc.gov/2021061994

2 4 6 8 10 9 7 5 3 1

New Directions Books are published for James Laughlin
by New Directions Publishing Corporation
80 Eighth Avenue, New York 10011

Chinatown

My watch reads ten o'clock. Vĩnh stretches and moans that he's sore. He's been sleeping on the Métro. His head on my shoulder. The train has stopped at some minor station. Fifteen minutes and still no sign of it moving. They have stumbled upon an abandoned duffel bag. They suspect a bomb in such a forlorn place is a ploy to mask a far more sinister scheme. I wonder if I should stay put and see just how sinister. Or leave and catch a bus. Vĩnh puts his head back on my shoulder and falls back asleep. At twelve the boy is as tall as Thụy was at sixteen. He eats lunch in the school cafeteria. One plate of mashed potato. One piece of fried steak. Two slices of jambon. Two slices of cheese. Yogurt. Ice cream. Cake. Thụy ate lunch at home. Home from school he would go straight to the kitchen to prepare lunch. Two cups of rice, half a bunch of morning glory, six brown shrimps for the three of them. Vĩnh is as tall as Thụy at sixteen. His hair is cropped like Thụy's hair. His eyes are slanted like Thụy's eyes. In class his friends call him that Chinese. In the streets people call him that Chinese. In the 13th arrondissement they address him in Cantonese. In school everybody called Thụy that Chink. Spawn of Deng Xiao Ping. Goon boy of Beijing. In the neighborhood everybody would see him and ask, hey when are you going back to your country. Have you sold all your furniture yet. The headmaster was summoned by the local police. Student Âu Phương Thụy should be watched closely.

3

Student Âu Phương Thụy's family have expressed their wish to stay in Vietnam. The higher-ups are still deliberating. The higher-ups have not yet made up their mind. But it's our duty to ensure that he is watched closely. The party congress has decreed that Beijing is enemy number one of the Vietnamese people. Student Âu Phương Thụy should be watched closely. The family might not have shown any signs yet. But it's our duty to ensure that he is watched closely. After meeting with the police, the headmaster summoned a staff meeting. After meeting with the staff, the homeroom teacher summoned a student council meeting. The next day a murmur went through the whole class, that boy Thụy is a problem. The next day again a rumor went through the whole school, that boy Thụy's family is on the counterespionage police's watch list. That boy Thụy's family receives secret documents from Beijing all the time. In class no one talked to him. No teacher called him to the blackboard. The other students looked away when he walked by. He was left out of military classes. He was exempted from writing letters of solidarity to servicemen in the Spratly Islands. In the final year of high school even the worst-behaved students were admitted to the Communist Youth Union. Not Thụy. They didn't even mention him. They acted like they'd never heard of any Thụy. They acted like there was no Thụy in the class. At sixteen he was as tall as Vĩnh is now. His hair was cropped. His eyes were slanted. On the bus, he fell asleep with his head on my shoulder. He told me he was born in Yên Khê. We were born in the same year. Thụy three months and two days before me. The next day a murmur went through the whole class that I had fallen for Thụy. The next day again a rumor went through the whole school that I was bewitched by that Beijing goon. The headmaster summoned my parents. The homeroom teacher wanted a private word with me. The math teacher wanted a private word with me. The literature teacher wanted a private word with me. The English teacher wanted a private word with me. The secretary of the school youth union wanted a private word with me. You should focus on topping your class in the final exams. You should focus on getting the highest scores in the exit exams. You should focus on bringing honor to our school in the university exams. Some evoked responsibility to try and convince me. Some brought up exams to try and threaten me. No one even mentioned Thụy. No one seemed to have heard of him. My parents also acted as if they'd never heard of him. Not once in my three years at high school did my parents mention him. And not once in my five years at university in Russia. My father said, you should focus on getting your red diploma. My mother said, just get the red diploma and then you can do as you please. My parents both hoped I would forget Thụy. My parents have been hoping for the last twenty-three years that I will forget Thụy. Vĩnh stretches again. The sinister scheme is still waiting for the special forces to come and investigate it. I'm still wondering if we should stay or try to catch a bus instead. The other three passengers in the Métro car growl, will the train start again or not, at least let us know that much. Three hours a day on public transportation is no way to live. I turn and say I also spend three hours a day on public transportation. No one reacts. I add so does the guy, he also spends three hours a day on public transportation. Still they don't react. I say his name is too long for anyone to remember, even if one spells it out. There's no point anyway. Better to call him the guy. He often calls me from his office desk. He often calls me on my fifteen-minute lunch break. While I'm chewing my sandwich in the staff room. My doctor says it's stress. Public-transportation-induced stress. Three hours a day. Stress doesn't exist in the third world. Third-world people suffer from many life-threatening diseases but never from stress. Vietnam is a third-world country but Vietnam enjoys delicious fruit all year round. Vietnam is richly endowed with natural resources. Vietnam boasts of Hạ Long Bay, the wonder of the world, of Sài Gòn, the pearl of the Far Orient, of Marguerite Duras, the Goncourt laureate. Stress doesn't exist in the third world. Stress can only be cured by Vietnam. The guy has visited Vietnam twelve times. Eleven times traveling from north to south by Soviet motorbike. A true tây ba lô, a "backpack westerner." He lives like a tramp, until he is back in Charles de Gaulle in his shorts and undershirt only, his hair to his shoulders and covered in mosquito bites. In the Métro people look at him sideways. In Vietnamese hotels receptionists cast one look at him and sigh. Why do you torture yourself so, I ask him. You think you're better than me, he asks me. He asks me a lot of things. Do you miss your mom's lemonade after all this time. Can your dad still carry a bicycle upstairs. So is Vĩnh still having that sore throat. Paul here gave it to Arthur just yesterday. Do your colleagues have any good ideas for the end of the year. Mine suggest eating out. The Cyclo Restaurant. Now it's my turn to pick the place. I'll have Vĩnh's favorite, roast pigeon. Yamina is repeating a year so is she going to be in the same class with her brother Yasin. How is Mlle. Feng Xiao these days. Is she going back home to have Deng Xiao Ping reinterred soon. He asks me a lot of things. Not once does he mention Thụy. Not once. He acts like he's never heard of any Thụy. Going to Vietnam, he avoids booking the same flight as Vĩnh's. Coming back to France, he does the same. He's afraid of running into Thụy at the airport. I ask him a lot of things. Not once do I ask about his wife. Not once do I mention his private life. Neither of now nor of the past. I don't need to know. I tell myself I don't need to know. I tell myself I don't have the time to poke around in his private life. How many times a month Paul and Arthur see their mother, where and for how long, is not something I concern myself with. I don't know his office number. Every time I call his home I have to check my notebook. He hasn't moved in the last ten years. But still I have to check my notebook. Hey is everything alright. Are things well with your job. Anyone having a sore throat over there. Vĩnh wants to talk to Paul and Arthur. Now there are two possibilities. Either Vĩnh will talk to one of the boys, for thirty minutes. I'm paying for unlimited minutes between the banlieue and Paris proper. Or else: so both boys are out. That's alright. No big deal. No need to call back. Children's talk, you know. The guy can recite my home number, my school staff room number, my cell number, my neighbor's number, Mlle. Feng Xiao's number with his eyes closed. I changed my email address three times in the last three years. But he never makes a mistake and he doesn't need a notebook. Wanadoo, Club-internet, Liberty.surf. My first and Thụy's middle name. Thụy's first and my middle name. My last name and Thụy's. Thụy's last name and mine. I myself can't remember. I have to check my notebook. To him it's no sweat. He doesn't need a notebook and he never makes a mistake. Going away, or back to his old home in Rennes, he always writes to me. Hi there. It's Sunday, are you going to worship at Mlle. Feng Xiao's soon. Remember to drop by Tang Frères and pick up some pigeon for Vĩnh. That movie *The Quiet American* is out soon. Wait for me and we'll go see it together. You should just send Vĩnh to my place. My aunt will roast some birds for the boys. But he says he prefers to call me. You have such a sullen face but your voice is not so bad. Easy on the ears, even. Your French is a jumble of accents. There's Vietnamese. And then Soviet. And Hà Nội. And Leningrad. Five years studying English in Russia didn't score you a lectureship in Thanh Xuân University, but a post in a secondary school in a Parisian banlieue is good enough. Being a secondary school teacher trumps being a member of the five-million-strong club of the French unemployed. Your voice isn't so bad. Talking to you on the phone is less tiring than looking at your sullen face. Now that's very stressful. So do your forty-nine colleagues at school say the same thing. He says his only strength is a stubborn memory. He can rattle off my work history like it's nothing. Vĩnh and I can both forget our own birthdays. The guy, he remembers everything.

7

Remembers everything even without a notebook. Without a glance at the birth certificates, he knows that I was born in the national ob-gyn hospital, that Vĩnh was born in the Vietnam-Sweden children's hospital, 2.9 kilograms in weight, sixty centimeters from head to toes. Twelve years later, Vĩnh is a meter taller, weighs ten times more, shoe size 39. Twelve years later, at one p.m. on a Sunday, Vĩnh pestered me for some roast pigeon. He says roast pigeon is the height of Vietnamese cuisine, as plentiful in calories as his school cafeteria lunch. Going back to Vietnam for the summer or New Year, he mostly eats lunch in Tạ Hiện street. At the sight of him the server will produce three portions of roast pigeon and one portion of fried rice. The waiter knows that he won't eat pickled glittering chive, that he likes Coke but not Tsingtao beer. Coke by Hà Nội brewery company in partnership with Tai Feng limited joint stock, for whom Vĩnh's grandmother is a branch representative. His grandmother who at the time he was born was counting the days until the end of the month to receive her early pension, along with his grandfather and their friends from Lương Ngọc Quyến street, nine men and nine women, twenty government workers all told who at the age of forty-five had been advised by the staff offices to submit their retirement letters. Twelve years later, one p.m. on a Sunday, I told Vĩnh, mom's so tired, your three roast pigeons marinated in húng lìu must wait until next week. He wailed, mom is always tired. If you're out of money, I'll lend you some. The money given to him by Thụy. I don't ever touch that money. Vĩnh says, I want to be independent. The moment I turn eighteen I'll get a job. The moment I turn eighteen I'll have a passport. A Vietnamese passport. A French passport. A Chinese passport. I will speak three languages. By then Chinese will be more powerful than English. Un milliard de chinois. Et moi. Et moi. Et moi, I tease him. I know he loves to be teased so. I knew he would soon fall asleep. He is still tired from going parachuting with Paul and Arthur yesterday.

Those two proposed a tour of duty in Iraq six years from now. Vĩnh waved a dismissive hand. Six years from now, regardless of whether the war in Iraq is still going on, he will parachute into Baghdad armed with his Chinese passport. Six years is enough for Chinese businesses to overtake American and British competitors, for his grandmother's Tai Feng joint stock to have opened dozens more branches in the Gulf states. Six years from now I will be forty-five. Thụy will be forty-five. There's another twenty years of teaching in store for me, so as to qualify for a Ministry of Education pension when I come to the end of my days. Who knows what's in store for Thụy, whether Hong Kong or Iraq, US or Rwanda. Six years from now Thụy's Chinese tongue will have grown sixfold in value. Six years from now Thụy's Âu clan will have grown sixfold in population. Vĩnh is asleep. I'm fast asleep beside him. I'm considering having a dream about Thụy and me, hand in hand going to receive our pension, when the guy calls. His call wakes us both up. I don't need to answer to know that it's him. Four p.m. on a Sunday. He'll keep calling me as long as he doesn't drop dead, as he likes to caveat. Four p.m. every Sunday. Even if he's away on vacation. Even if he's back home in Rennes. Even if it's raining all day long where he is, or the temperature reaches thirty-five degrees, and the sea just a little distance away with its green green water and gentle waves. Even under the sun of Củ Chi, Yên Bái, Cà Mau. Four p.m. every Sunday. He knows all telephone operators. He knows how to say chào anh chào chị when he arrives. Chào anh chào chị when he leaves. Hotel receptionists look at him and sigh but the small province operators, piping thuốc lào tobacco from morning till night, find him quaintly cute. The small province operators know him as mister Frenchman. Come on in mister Frenchman have a cup of tea. I see you've come to call your girlfriend again mister Frenchman. It's already 2004 but the phrase "tây ba lô" hasn't traveled far from Hà Nội and Sài Gòn. In Củ Chi, Yên Bái, Cà Mau, people are still innocent enough to assume every mister Frenchman is a capitalist. How could a noncapitalist afford to talk for ten minutes at the rate of two hundred thousand đồng. Two hundred thousand đồng can't get you a ticket to see a diva duet by Thanh Lam and Hồng Nhung in either Hà Nội or Sài Gòn, but two hundred thousand đồng gets you forty kilograms of maize in Yên Bái, forty kilograms of cassava roots in Củ Chi, forty kilograms of flour in Rạch Giá. The last time he called, it was from an Internet café in Hàm Long street. Last year, two hundred thousand đồng got you a ten-minute call to the EU. This year, competition between the new military- and the old state-owned companies means we enjoy half the rate. There are five Internet cafés in Hàm Long street alone. He waged a shouting match with three other people who were also placing calls to the EU. His French throat held no candle to their Vietnamese ones, so I heard two calls to Germany and a third one to France. They were each discussing their children's imminent overseas studies. Each agonizing over who there will be for a returning French or German speaker to talk to, in which company a French or German degree will be accepted. Each agreeing heartily that a French or German college is much cheaper than a Vietnamese one. There's no such thing as Teachers' Day in French or German calendars, so parents won't have to catch a Vietnam Airlines plane over there to celebrate, to haul some offerings of oranges to their children's French or German professors. Four p.m. in Hà Nội. Eleven a.m. in Paris. Eleven a.m., a summer day in Paris. I was wrapped in blankets. He was in shorts and tank top braving the thirty-nine-degree heat. I cradled the receiver, listening to his shouting match. Twenty minutes in, his voice was already hoarse. The other three would be shouting for another ten minutes several times over. He says he prefers calling to writing emails. You have such a sullen face but your voice is not so bad. You mix four accents like hodgepodge fried rice but I can understand it. It's not so bad. Easy on the ears even. Four p.m. on a Sunday. I don't need to answer to know that it's him. At his first hi I already know he will propose running three laps around Belleville park. I wave a dismissive hand. Vĩnh and I are both busy. Vĩnh's grandmother is over for a meeting with the Tai Feng branch representative in France. His grandmother brings him a crate of Coca-Cola to wash down his roast pigeon. His grandmother says that when he goes back to Vietnam again she will give him another crate to go, together with three Tạ Hiện roast pigeons to eat on the plane. One plate of Vietnam Airlines fried rice and two slices of Vietnamese ham stuffed with flour and MSG cannot provide the plentiful calories the boy needs. The guy says then I can just stay at home and provide calories for Vĩnh's grandmother. He hangs up. Without even saying goodbye. Whenever he goes to Hà Nội he drops by my place without fail, and without fail my parents seize the opportunity to gripe at how Vĩnh and I are neglected by Thụy and his parents. Whenever their homeland gift arrives without fail it comes with a letter, and the letter comes with a question as to when he and I will get married, when I will bring him back to Vietnam to introduce him to all our relatives. Doing the rounds of the relatives is the point. After twelve visits to Vietnam he understands that all too well. After twelve visits to Vietnam he now knows enough to make excuses to my parents. So that my parents can later make excuses to the relatives: One of them has just started at a new school. The other has just started at a new job. One is studying for a second degree. The other is abroad on a business trip. His dear father has some ailment. His kind mother doesn't feel so well. Last year Vĩnh went back to Vietnam. The return trip cost six hundred euros. His pocket money another hundred. Half my monthly wage. His paternal grandparents cannot give him half my monthly wage but they did drive all the way to the airport to pick him up. Also for a round of their own set of relatives. His Vietnamese leaves much to be desired. But the Chinese yes sir no ma'am roll right off his tongue.

His tongue is still made for Tạ Hiện roast pigeon. He knows current affairs in the PRC like the back of his hand. His paternal grandparents know that my secondary teacher's wage cannot stretch to a house in the 13th arrondissement. But every Wednesday afternoon Vĩnh goes to rue Tolbiac for his Chinese class. The Chinese spoken in the 13th arrondissement is not Beijingese, but even Beijingers don't speak Beijingese anymore. Like Hanoians don't speak Hanoiese. His paternal grandparents find nothing in him to complain about, and nothing in me. They never complain about me. Ever. They came all the way to the maternity ward to pick me up. His father carrying the baby in the front. His mother holding my hand in the back. His father named the baby Vĩnh. Father is Thụy. Son is Vĩnh. Vĩnh Thụy would have been sacrilegious once. His mother was unsure about the name. His father said Vĩnh means everlasting in Chinese. Father Âu Phương Thụy. Son Âu Phương Vĩnh. Later when a baby girl comes along she will be named Hằng. Hằng has the same meaning as Vĩnh. Hằng is as beautiful a name as Vĩnh. His parents talked of the future. Grandson Vĩnh. Granddaughter Hằng. Family planning in the People's Republic of China is twice as exact as that in the Socialist Republic of Vietnam. In the future Chinese girls would be hard to come by. In the future Chinese girls would be free to have their pick. Hằng, surnamed Âu, slanted eyes, speaking Chinese. Whether she holds a Chinese passport is irrelevant. Un milliard de chinois. Et moi. Et moi. Et moi. By the time she comes of age, those billion Chinese will have become a billion and a half. China will have become a country without borders. Hằng and Vĩnh can go wherever they like without fear of losing their roots, their language, their Tạ Hiện roast pigeon. Thụy's parents talked of the future. Thụy's parents handed Vĩnh and me over to my parents. A week after I left the hospital. We find nothing in you to complain about, girl. If things don't work out between the two of you, don't blame us. I never do blame Thụy's parents. And I never blame Thụy.

After twelve years my missing him has yet to run its course. I let the guy travel north to south alone on a Soviet motorbike as a backpack westerner living like a tramp, coming back to Charles de Gaulle in shorts and undershirt only. The day we went to the airport to pick Vĩnh up, the guy's hair still came to his shoulders. His skin was still covered in mosquito bites. I asked him, don't you think it's time you stop torturing yourself. He asked me, do you think you're better than me. Without so much as a hello Vĩnh declared, what an awful haircut mom has, stop giving Mlle. Feng Xiao so much liberty. Indicating the boy by his side he said, this is my good friend Hao Peng. I'd heard a lot about Hao Peng. The two boys were in the same class in rue Tolbiac. They had arranged to meet in the Bangkok airport waiting area. Vĩnh flew from Hà Nội. Hao Peng from Beijing. During the twelve-hour flight back to Paris, Hao Peng had given Vĩnh a full tour of the PRC. These days, in Shanghai you feel like you're in Chicago. You never see a beggar singing for money in the brand-new, smooth-sailing underground. In Guangdong they just wrapped up the biggest bribery trial ever, five got death and ten got life. Next month in Kunming they're unveiling the world's largest nuclear power plant. Last year in Beijing Chairman Jiang Ze Min himself inaugurated the international mathematics festival. Guangdong has earned a spot in the *Guinness Book of Records* for the highest number of luxury restaurants per capita, coupled with the highest number of roast pigeons sold every month. In my Hangzhou a floating hotel has just been built, with every room opening to its own golf course, its own outdoor swimming pool higher than sea level. In your Hunan things are also very smart these days. A six-lane flyover is said to be in development, reaching from the municipal people's committee headquarters all the way to Tian'anmen. In Mlle. Feng Xiao's Sichuan they are preparing a grand ceremony for the tenth anniversary of Deng Xiao Ping's demise, so the province plans to import eight million little jars to build a memorial for their homonym-sake, the greatest former chairman of China. After twelve hours, Vĩnh's heart was already drumming in his chest. By the time the airplane landed, he had found Hao Peng to be the worthiest of all his Paris friends. Hao Peng, who's never late for class. Hao Peng, who speaks proper Mandarin. Hao Peng, who translates from Chinese to French even faster than the teacher. Hao Peng, who bagged the gold medal in the municipal youth's table tennis tournament last year. Hao Peng, who says an exemplary Chinese youth has to be well-rounded, agile in body and sharp in mind. Hao Peng, who went straight from the barber shop to the airport. PRC shampoo and PRC hair spray. I waited for the guy at the gate of Belleville park. PRC shampoo and PRC hair spray. He made no comment. He always avoids commenting on my appearance. Half an hour and a lap round the park later, he asked if Mlle. Feng Xiao was well. I mumbled yes. Then he asked if Mlle. Feng Xiao had told me anything interesting. He asks about Mlle. Feng Xiao whenever he wants to make me laugh. My hair has been Mlle. Feng Xiao's to cut, wash, and spray for the last ten years. Mlle. Feng Xiao entertains her clients with many a delightful story. Her Vietnamese is not much better than Vĩnh's, but she has cute canines and dimpled cheeks. I spend less time listening to her than I do admiring her looks. I always feel like I understand everything she says. On the first day, upon my confessing that I was fresh from Vietnam, she smiled, so nǐ are a Yuenanese. I instantly warmed up to her. Thụy used to tease me saying I was Yuenan folk. Yuenan was once a province of China. Taking up with him, I would have no fear of losing my roots. A year later I found out that she is an Âu too. An Âu like Thụy. Like Vĩnh. Âu Feng Xiao. Âu Phương Thụy. Âu Phương Vĩnh. If Thụy hadn't boarded the Thống Nhất, we would have had Âu Phương Hằng. Chinese girls will be very desirable in the future. Mlle. Feng Xiao turns fifty this year. Mlle. Feng Xiao lives her unmarried life with her sister who will be sixty in two years. The two mesdemoiselles went all the way from Sichuan to Paris. Sichuan lies in the west of China, a thousand kilometers from Beijing. Sichuan is the homeland of Deng Xiao Ping. Mlle. Feng Xiao recounted how when Deng Xiao Ping turned his back on Mao Ze Dong, becoming a party outcast, in her village they smashed all their little jars to smithereens and threw the shards into the pond. Four million people in the whole province of Sichuan smashed eight million little jars. Feeling that was not enough, they imported jars from neighboring provinces so that they had more to smash. Two for adults, one for children. I was a child, I was also given one. I smashed it even harder than my older siblings did theirs. But now the eight million people of Sichuan all know that it was thanks to Deng Xiao Ping that China could become what it is today. The eight million people of Sichuan wept the hardest the day he passed away. He passed away, poor fellow. In ailments and agony. Poor fellow. Mlle. Feng Xiao says her Vietnamese has gotten so much better since she met me. Vietnamese and Chinese tongues are so close. Seeing me once a month is enough for her to be fluent in Vietnamese. Vietnam and China are so close too. Seeing me once a month is enough for her to know that what there is in her land is also there in mine. I find Mlle. Feng Xiao charming. I have had few opportunities to get close to the local Chinese community. I can hardly run to them, grasp their hands and say, my husband is also ethnically Chinese. I'm an Âu. My only son Vĩnh is an Âu. When he turns eighteen he will have three nationalities. When he turns eighteen he will go to the Gulf as a branch representative of Tai Feng JSC and arrange an interpreter's job for me in Baghdad. Every first Sunday of the month Vĩnh is deposited at one of my neighbors' while I go visit Mlle. Feng Xiao. He says, mom goes to Mlle. Feng Xiao the way people go to church. Mlle. Feng Xiao is the only Chinese I know in Paris. Mlle. Feng Xiao is an Âu. She came from Sichuan. Her hometown lies to the west of Beijing, a thousand kilometers away. Thụy has no hometown. His filial ancestors were born in Hunan. His great-grandfather was born in Hunan. His grandfather was born in Hunan. But he was born in Yên Khê. At sixteen, a high school graduate, he took the entrance exams for the Polytechnic University but was assigned to the University of Architecture instead. With Chinese gunners threatening to fire five cannonballs a day over the border with Vietnam, the Vietnamese government would hear nothing of ethnically Chinese doctors and engineers. And with the Vietnamese government receiving a thousand Soviet prefab houses every quarter, the student body at Hà Nội University of Architecture was made up solely of country hicks with only a pencil to their name. Studying architecture still trumped studying how to plant a forest or cure buffalo of hoof disease. After five years, once your hands had come to know their way around the pencil, you could find some job to escape to, and even a janitor's or a typist's post was a good escape, today's country hick being much more flexible than today's city slicker. At sixteen I got into Thanh Xuân University, where I learned Russian. At seventeen I departed for Leningrad. My future was wide open. At the airport my father recited in a loud singsong voice, O Russia, thou art my children's paradise. My mother said Tố Hữu's poetry is so fine, his verses are happy and they also rhyme. All they wanted was that I would be happy. All they hoped was that paradisiacal Russia would make me forget Thụy. Thụy didn't come to the airport to see me off. He had never been allowed inside my parents' house. My father would answer the door saying that I was busy studying. My mother would answer the door saying that I had a headache. Then came my dizziness, my toothache, my sore throat. It didn't take long before he got the message. He didn't come again. I went into the public bathroom, wanting to have a good cry. The public bathroom in Nội Bài airport twenty-three years ago was on par with the one in Thanh Xuân University. Twenty-three emerald-green bottle flies meant I couldn't shed a single nostalgic tear over

Thụy. At seventeen, I had not yet known what five years feels like. At twenty-seven, having been through a five-year span twice over, I got married to Thụy. At thirty-seven, after twice that five-year time again, I had been without him for nine years altogether. At thirty-seven, I was already a veteran teacher for the Ministry of Education, he a veteran architect for the whole Chinese community in Chợ Lớn. His Chinese tongue is very desirable now. His Âu surname is also very desirable now. His Chinese tongue, which had no use whatsoever when we got married. His Âu surname, which was in the Hà Nội police's blacklist when we got married. The first time I told her about him, my mother said, the Chinese are inscrutable. I don't believe him to be inscrutable. I don't blame his parents. I never blame his parents. His parents, who welcomed a grandson and immediately looked forward to a granddaughter. His parents, who came all the way to the maternity ward to pick me up. His father carrying baby Vĩnh in the front. His mother holding my hand in the back. His parents went all the way to the airport to pick Vĩnh up. Summer or New Year holiday all the same. His parents find nothing in me to complain about. His parents have nothing to blame me for. His mother came to France for a weeklong meeting. We took photographs at my place, using up a whole Kodak roll of thirty-six exposures. His father wrote me a letter full of praise, the two of you staying in that place is very good. Belleville cannot yet become a part of the 13th arrondissement, but Belleville is very good. Even on a side street you find ten restaurants, five clothing stores, two leather goods stores. If you squint, you'll even find a money exchange shop. If you squint really hard, you'll even find a shop sign saying "Âu." And if you squint until your eyes are nothing but thin slits, you'll find that the telephone number is the only thing that tells you it's not a shop sign in Hong Kong. His parents find nothing in me to complain about. They understand that I give him my all. Since the first time they met me twenty-three years ago, they already understood that I would give him my all. Belleville cannot yet be a part of the 13th arrondissement, but the rent in Belleville is half what they pay in the 13th. In Belleville even on a side street you find ten restaurants, five clothing stores, two leather goods stores. Living in Belleville on your secondary teacher's wage is very good. In the future, when Vĩnh goes to the Gulf as a branch representative, you can move to the 13th arrondissement no problem. In the 13th arrondissement, even in tour Olympiades where Mlle. Feng Xiao lives, a one-bedroom apartment costs 700 euros. On the eighteenth floor, five times a week, the shuttling elevators are halted right at high noon by a power outage. Right at high noon the whole eighteenth floor, in concert with the other seventeen floors, must complete ten thousand nem, twenty thousand bánh cuốn, three thousand har gow. At the order of a hundred ethnic deli spécialités chinoises et vietnamiennes. Ninety-nine of which have Chinese owners, as a matter of fact. The hundredth is currently owned by a Vietnamese, but a Chinese owner is already finalizing its purchase. In the 13th arrondissement, in the very tour Olympiades where Mlle. Feng Xiao lives, you can wait for a year before someone announces that their apartment is up for sale. But without any such announcement, people are already lining up to buy. To pay in hard cash. Never mind going through the Real Estate Municipal Department. Never mind registering at some people's committee. And the very next day there's a new haircut-and-perm shop. A bridal shop, makeup and rental gowns. A tailor shop, suits for men and suits for women, Shanghai cheongsams and ballroom dresses. Next month if there's no new piece to be tailored, the space can be converted to an office. A travel agency. A marriage therapy clinic. A hothouse for vegetables. A private kindergarten. A real estate office. A wholesale store, from whence every day a thousand leather coats, a thousand leather briefcases, a thousand pairs of leather shoes go forth to Paris and the surrounding areas. Thụy's parents understand that I give him my all.

They don't need to consult my Purple Star chart. They understood it the first time they met me. After a year as their daughter-in-law, and then a week staying at their place when Vĩnh was born, I'd learned how to prepare ten Chinese holiday dishes. How the Chinese use soy sauce instead of fish sauce. Even boiled green vegetables are seasoned with sesame sauce and sugar. I learned how the Chinese, once they trust someone, trust them unto death. How Chinese wives never turn their backs on their men. I never turn my back on Thụy. Vĩnh was one month old when Thụy said he'd had it up to here with Hà Nội. In Hà Nội there were only ten ethnically Chinese families left. Ten ethnically Chinese families, who huddled up in Lương Ngọc Quyến street. Ten ethnically Chinese families, who had faith in the party. Ten ethnically Chinese families, whose children would never become doctors or engineers. The party only needed engineers and doctors with family names like Nguyễn, or Trần, or Lê. Thụy, saddled with a name like Âu, had no choice but to leave, to head south for Chợ Lớn. Chợ Lớn, where ten thousand ethnically Chinese families lived. Chợ Lớn, which—after all the merging and splitting—was still a part of Sài Gòn. The party was also more open-minded when it came to Sài Gòn. Engineers and doctors who were a Nguyễn, a Lê, a Trần from Hà Nội kept being sent to Sài Gòn to serve, but demand remained high. Engineers and doctors who were a Nguyễn, a Lê, a Trần from Sài Gòn, ten years after South and North were united under the same roof, had mostly exported themselves to the US, or France, or Australia, or Canada. The Soviet experts had not yet designed prefab houses for Sài Gòn so architects were still needed, and the party decided that a country hick architect, an ethnically Chinese architect was at least more trustworthy than one from the imposter government or army who architected their Independence Palace or their American embassy. So, one by one, the ten ethnically Chinese families of Lương Ngọc Quyến street entrusted their children to the ten thousand ethnically Chinese families of Sài Gòn in Chợ Lớn. Thụy'd had it up to here with Hà Nội. He only took a single change of clothes. His degree from the University of Architecture was left to Hà Nội. He walked to Hàng Cỏ station. He boarded the eleven p.m. Thống Nhất. That's all I knew about his departure. After that, where he was, whom he met, what he did. I didn't know a thing. On Vĩnh's very first birthday, he wrote home. Two hundred thousand đồng plus a black-and-white photograph. He was standing by a two-story house, a shop sign with Chinese lettering, a pair of Chinese lanterns. I didn't know where he was, whom he met, what he did, in those days. Two years later I watched Duras follow her lover into Chợ Lớn. In every street, two-story houses. Two-story houses, shop signs with Chinese lettering, pairs of lanterns. I didn't know where he was, whom he met, what he did. Even now I still don't know where he was, whom he met, what he did. For the last twelve years I have been wanting to see him, to ask. How he is living his life now. I don't need to know. But I want to know where he was, whom he met, what he did, in those days. The two-story house, the shop sign with Chinese lettering, the pair of lanterns. In those days. In those days, Vĩnh was just one month old. The baby learned how to roll over. How to crawl. How to walk. Thụy was nowhere in sight. The baby cut a tooth. Got weaned. Got measles. Thụy was nowhere in sight. He got bitten on the ear by red ants and ran a thirty-nine-degree fever for an entire week. Thụy was nowhere in sight. He swallowed a rambutan stone and had to be rushed to the Vietnam-Sweden children's hospital. Thụy was nowhere in sight. He was bitten on the nose by another boy in the kindergarten, then made to face the wall, the teacher's punishment for the Beijing goon who dared bully a Vietnamese commoner. Thụy was nowhere in sight. Thụy was nowhere in sight. For the last twelve years I have been wanting to see him, to ask. Vĩnh and I arrived at the airport in the torrential rain. I ran into the public bathroom.

The same bathroom from the day I left for Russia. Twelve years had gone by but the number of emerald-green bottle flies remained unchanged. But I now knew how separation feels. My mother stood outside, holding baby Vĩnh. I stood inside, crying. I wanted to see Thụy to ask. I wanted to call off the whole trip just for a chance to see him. I only wanted to ask him how it had been in those days. How he was living his life now, I didn't need to know. My mother pounded on the door. I hadn't finished crying yet. My mother pounded harder. I cried harder. Vĩnh cried harder. My father tried to joke, cry even harder, grandpa will take a photo of crybaby and crymama. My father wanted to include my mother in the photo. But my mother said it's taboo to take a photo of three. The middle one will suffer from bad luck. Again my father joked, then let me be the middle man. To see Paris and die, that's the worst that can happen, no. O Paris, thou art my children's paradise. My father recited in a loud singsong voice. My father said Tố Hữu's poetry is still happy and still rhymes. But Tố Hữu had gotten it wrong. By the end of the twentieth century Russia had turned into hell. Capitalism is the real paradise. He rambled on about all kinds of things. He ran out for some biscuits for Vĩnh. He gave the baby a shoulder ride all over the airport. Vĩnh was no longer crying. He was wearing what his paternal grandparents gave him a few days back for his birthday. His paternal grandparents didn't come to the airport. Grandpa was occupied. Grandma was unwell. My mother didn't want Thụy's parents to come to the airport either. She said traveling was a pain. I knew my mother didn't want to see his parents. Again I ran into the public bathroom. The long line drove me out. My mother was making a fuss, hurry up you still have to go and check in your baggage. I walked, but my feet didn't seem to touch the ground. I carried Vĩnh onto the plane. The two air hostesses drew up the ladder. I had a glimpse of my parents waving from afar. In my mother's hand was the handkerchief I'd left in the public bathroom. In my father's was the packet of biscuits Vĩnh hadn't finished. I only wanted to see Thụy to ask. I wanted to call off the whole trip just for a chance to see him. Where he was, whom he met, what he did, in those days. The two-story house, the shop sign with Chinese lettering, the pair of lanterns. In those days. I lay holding Vĩnh in my arms. The eighteen-square-meter apartment in the Đê La Thành blocks. The double bed in the innermost corner. By its side was the bookshelf Thụy made for me. In the middle of the room, the small table with the couple of little stools, also made by him. He and I sat there for tea in the mornings. I read to him from books in the late afternoons. I told him about Leningrad. The white nights. The Neva. The moving bridges. The winters without him. I wanted to call off the whole trip. Just to see him. Just to ask him where he was, whom he met, what he did, in those days. How he was living his life now, I didn't need to know. But I wanted to know how it had been in those days. I climbed up into the plane, eyes brimming with tears. In the torrential rain. The guy sat beside us on the plane. He was fresh from a guided tour around Hà Nội, Huế, Hội An. He said he didn't go on southward to Sài Gòn. He reached as far as Hội An and then went back. Hội An was pretty but he didn't like it there. Huế was pretty but he didn't like it there. Hà Nội was not as pretty but he liked it there. He talked nonstop. He didn't give me a chance to nod off. Later, he said he had seen me run into the public bathroom twice. He didn't mention my crying while my mother pounded on the door. He didn't mention my almost losing a bag because I kept running every two minutes to look toward the airport gate. He didn't mention my remembering my passport was still in my father's briefcase only when I was in front of the immigrant officer. I once asked him, did my eyes swell to the size of oranges. He said vaguely, was that so, I didn't really pay attention. He always avoids commenting on my appearance. He sat beside us on the plane. He talked nonstop. He didn't give me a chance to nod off. He didn't give me a chance to

22

miss Thụy. He talked about shopping in the flea market in Trần Cao Vân street. He talked about playing games of chess by Hoàn Kiếm lake. He talked about eating snakes in Lệ Mật village. The snake's heart submerged in a cup of rice wine was still beating after five minutes. The snake's head was chopped finely and turned into meatballs. The snake's sides were put into nem. The snake's back was taken out and mixed into salad. The snake's belly was cooked in a soup with scallions and coriander. The snake's skin was fried until swollen and eaten in a roll with broken rice crackers. The snake's tail was stewed in mung bean soup with coconut milk. Nothing was wasted. It was incredible. He seemed to have taken a liking to Lệ Mật village. He seemed to have taken a liking to the seven-course snake. He told me a lot of things. Things wholly outside the program of the guided tour. Things he'd never had anyone to tell. Later, he said my face had looked so sullen then. But for some reason he kept talking. Kept talking without even checking if I was listening. Or if I liked it. He was like the black to Thụy's white. He always tells me where he stays, whom he meets, what he does, without prompt. He sat beside us on the plane. He acted the clown to make us laugh. He cracked jokes about those who were on his guided tour. He called them the trade officials. The trade officials screamed and shrieked at any trivial thing. They saw a lizard and took it for a viper. They saw pork and assumed it was dogmeat. They saw a cockroach and retched their guts out. They saw a mosquito and nearly emptied their spray bottles of repellent. They saw a bee and ran like their lives depended on it. They saw a spider and screamed loud enough to bring down the house. The trade officials took a diarrhea pill on leaving their hotel. They took a diarrhea pill when visiting the Confucian Temple. They took a diarrhea pill in the middle of their lunch. They took a diarrhea pill listening to a quan họ concert. They jerked awake from a dream on their hospital beds and took a diarrhea pill. He talked nonstop. He made my ears ache. He made my nerves tense. He spared me no time to miss Thụy. In the course of a three-hour flight, he managed to make me and Vĩnh laugh three times. He took some paper and made the boy a ship and a plane. He asked the air hostess to please warm some water for me and some milk for Vĩnh. He suggested that the gentleman in front might perhaps raise his seat a little. He apologized to the lady in the row behind when Vĩnh took her glasses by mistake. He talked nonstop. He wiggled all the time. During our layover in Bangkok I thought I would be able to shake him off for two hours. For two hours, my brain wouldn't have to grapple with French words. For two hours, my brain would be free to miss Thụy as much as I liked. After all the years, I still wanted to see him. To ask where he'd gone, whom he'd met, what he'd done. In those days. I still kept in my bag the piece of paper that he'd signed. That my mother had dictated and my father typed up. I hadn't had the nerve to hand it to his parents. In tears, I'd asked his younger sister to give it to him. I hadn't known his address. I had never set foot in Sài Gòn. And I'd never even heard of Chợ Lớn. The police said that without the father's approval, they couldn't put Vĩnh's information on my passport. My father said, you should focus hard on your studies. No more "while you're still young" as I was going on thirty. My mother said, come back from France and then you can do as you please. You put so much effort into passing your exams. My parents hoped that paradisiacal Paris would make me forget Thụy. My parents have been hoping for the last twenty-three years that I will forget Thụy. I told them I wouldn't go anywhere on my own. Vĩnh was not even two yet. He was all that was left to me. All that was left to me by which to remember Thụy. He came to resemble Thụy more with each passing day. Down to the last toenail. Every time she saw him his grandmother would exclaim, the handle always resembles the basket. In tears I asked Thụy's sister to give him the piece of paper. No letter to go along with it. I didn't understand why I hadn't written a letter. There were so many things I wanted to ask but I didn't write a letter. His sister also remarked on it, you didn't write a letter. I didn't answer. That day too there was torrential rain. Inside me it was all a mist. The bureau for university cooperation had called me to their office. If my passport was not ready by the end of the month, it would be too late for the visa. I might not arrive in time to meet with an advisor, to be assigned a topic. My father wouldn't touch his food. My mother wouldn't stop weeping. The house was like a house in mourning. One month before my scheduled departure. Inside me it was all a mist. I didn't need Thụy to sign that piece of paper. I didn't need his two hundred thousand đồng. I just wanted to ask where he'd gone, whom he'd met, what he'd done. In those days. In those days. My uncle said to my mother, let me go have a good talk to that man's parents. My aunt said, let me go give them a good threat. But in the end it wasn't necessary. That night, in the torrential rain, his sister knocked on my door. At the bottom of the piece of paper that my mother had dictated and my father typed up, there was his signature. That was all there was in the big envelope. No letter. No photograph. No two hundred thousand đồng. Inside me it was all a mist. His sister said, do you need anything else. I didn't answer. I didn't understand a thing. I didn't say goodbye as she left. I didn't look at the piece of paper. All I saw was his signature. One month before my scheduled departure. The torrential rain endured. I didn't need his signature. I just wanted to ask him how it had been. In those days. As for that piece of paper, my father turned it into many Xerox copies. My mother sent one to the bureau for university cooperation, took one to the notary and translation service, brought one to the local police, put one in the drawer with our most important papers. She also gave one to me. Inside me it was all a mist. I just wanted to see Thụy. To ask him how it had been in those days. I sat in the Bangkok airport with Vĩnh in my arms. In my bag was Thụy's photograph. The two-story house, the shop sign with Chinese lettering, the pair of lanterns. Later, I heard Duras describe the din of Chợ Lớn. I understood everything. But I didn't understand a thing. With wariness I read Duras's words. I had not set foot in Sài Gòn. I knew nothing about Chợ Lớn. I read *The Lover* and watched the movie. I even read *The North China Lover*. I heard Duras describe the smells of Chợ Lớn. Agarwood, watermelons, restaurants. I read Duras's every word wondering if I was being duped. I just wanted to know where he'd gone, whom he'd met, what he'd done. In those days. The two-story house, the shop sign with Chinese lettering, the pair of lanterns. I sat in the Bangkok airport with Vĩnh in my arms. Thụy's signature in my bag. The torrential rain outside. Inside me it was all a mist. Out of the blue the guy ran to us, producing a coconut milk for me and two apples for Vĩnh. From then on, until we boarded the plane, he was silent. He was silent for the next twelve hours. Vĩnh slept in his arms. The gentleman in front thoughtfully raised his seat a little. The lady behind turned off her reading light. The air hostesses sat nodding in a corner. Dimness filled the plane's interior. I took out Thụy's signature and studied it. He had not put a date. A date for me to know that on that day of that month he had thought of me, of Vĩnh. Never did he write to me. The eighteen-square-meter apartment in the Đê La Thành blocks. The bookshelf on the wall. The small table with the couple of stools in the middle of the room. The cupboard in the kitchen. All made by him. I read to him from books. I told him about Leningrad. The white nights. Nevsky Prospect. The Neva. Dostoyevsky. He said he loved *Crime and Punishment*. I said the Russian winter was sad. In Leningrad even more so. So cold your ears fell off. It snowed even in May. I had no news from him. Letters to him were sent without reply. My parents wrote every month without ever mentioning him. My worst nightmare was that I would never meet him again. I fell on the way to class. I had to stay at home for a month. For the whole month I dreamed that Thụy was ill. He was taken to the hospital, but no one would treat him. They saw his Âu name on the registration form and said, you might as well go home. I read *Crime and Punishment*, in which the main character killed himself. Now I worried that Thụy would grow despondent and tired of life. In the summer of my third year, I spent my holidays picking fruit in the countryside. I got three hundred rubles, so I wrote home, I'm coming home this winter holiday. Three weeks later, a letter arrived from my mother. Everybody's well. Everything's as usual. The other day I and your father passed by Lương Ngọc Quyến street. The ten Chinese families had got on the train to Quảng Ninh, they must be in Hong Kong by now. I never forgave my mother. My last year and a half in Russia was the most dejected year and a half of my life. Later, I had Vĩnh with me. I had known love. I had reasons to live. But back then I was twenty-one. Russia was sad and cold. So cold your ears fell off. It snowed even in May. I had no news from Thụy. Later I often asked why he didn't write to me. He smiled but said nothing. Later, lying by his side at night, I still dreamed that they turned him away from the hospital, that he fell, that blood pooled under his head. Later, waiting until dark for him to come home, I was scared that someone would come pounding on the door to tell me he had taken his life. His taking his own life was my greatest fear. Hanging himself, drinking insecticide, jumping from a train. I didn't dare pursue the thought. Lying by his side, I didn't dare pursue those thoughts. Every dream of mine was a catastrophe. Every catastrophe ended in his death. In the year we lived together, I gave him my all. I wanted to forget all about the days in Leningrad. I wanted to forget the letter from my mother. I wanted to forget my canceled plane ticket. Russia was as cold as ice. It snowed even in May. One by one, my girlfriends got married and had children. Or had children and got married. They figured that marriage before graduation had many advantages. To kid parents raising actual kids, any junk could pass

27

for food. After graduation, they would qualify for family-grade overseas shipping. Tripled allowance of things to go into their overseas crates. And a baby meant a one-year leave from school. A one-year extension of their stay in Russia. A day extended is a day gained. One by one they got married and I attended their weddings. To eat random junk passing for food. Nem stuffed with cabbage and beef meatballs. Cabbage salad with a sprinkling of walnut. Curry with cabbage, potatoes, and mutton. Russia was as cold as ice. It snowed even in May. Russia had no vegetable other than cabbage, but if the socialist bloc had not come tumbling down Russia would have remained paradise for students from Vietnam, Cuba, North Korea, Mongolia. One by one they had babies and I visited them in the maternity wards. One by one they packed their overseas crates and I watched them fuss. My own meagre crate consisted of a few dozen books, a fridge for my mother, a record player for my father. The day I got married to Thụy, my mother gave me back the fridge, my father said, take the player so that you have something to listen to. In our sparse love nest. A bookshelf on the wall. A small table with a couple of stools in the middle of the room. A cupboard in the kitchen. All made by him. He and I sat there for tea in the mornings. I put on a song for him. The player made a wheezing sound. Soviet records meeting the wet summer wind of Hà Nội were all ways of warped. Vĩnh was exactly one month old when Thụy said he'd had it up to here with Hà Nội. I could only do as he wished. I told him so. Hundreds of times over in that eighteen-square-meter apartment in the Đê La Thành blocks. In those days of love and pangs. Dimness filled the plane's interior. I studied his signature. The piece of paper that my mother had dictated and my father typed up. With Thụy's signature at the bottom. Without a date. A date for me to know that in that day of that month he had thought of me. His sister didn't tell me anything else. And I didn't ask. Neither did I write to him. Even now I still don't understand why I didn't write to him. At the time, writing seemed impossible. I didn't know what to write. I didn't know how to bare my heart in writing. I had never kept a diary. Not even in the frostiest days in Leningrad. But I don't understand why I didn't write to him. Inside me it was all a mist. I was afraid that I would have nothing to write to him. And that he would have nothing to write to me. It's been twelve years, and I still don't understand any of it. It's been twelve years, and I still haven't dared write to him. It's been twelve years, and now I vaguely understand that one can't simply take up a pen and write.

I'm Yellow

Night. Night is yellow, the color of that single small bulb in the corridor. I stare into the night. I throw the key into the night. It makes no sound in the yellow of the night.

I walk. Not because I haven't been out on the streets for quite a while. Not because the yellow of night is ever absent from my canvas. Because I have no other means of transport. My bike I've left to Loan. Along with the apartment. And the fifty paintings I have been churning out over the last fifty days. They are, of course, of no artistic value. What they are is the guarantee of a comfortable life for Loan and our daughter for the next five years. I don't hate myself for producing those paintings. Nor do I hate my wife, who made me do it. My own apathy surprises me. But I must leave. I've been preparing for this taking leave for the last fifty days, a painting a day, each properly numbered.

I walk through the streets of yellow.

Tomorrow I turn thirty-nine.

Five years ago, I put an end to my bachelor's life with a wedding. Such a stupid thing to have done. As early as the nuptial night, lying by her side, I had known that it was such a stupid thing. Our married life lasted five years. During those five years Loan gave me a beautiful baby girl. During those five years I gave Loan and our daughter five hundred paintings. They were, of course, of no artistic value. Like the fifty I produced in the last fifty days, what they were was the guarantee of a comfortable life for us. This was the contract made between the two us, as early as the nuptial night. Loan would be in charge of the spiritual side of our marriage, I the material. Our daughter, conceived three months after that night, also had her role in our three-way contract. She was to be the overseer, reminding us both not to neglect our respective duties. And fifty-three days ago, when I decided to leave, in other words to break our contract, she was the one who sat in the middle of the courtroom, with me, the accused, on one side, and her mother, the victim, on the other, obliging me to renounce all properties, movable or immovable, together with fifty paintings, whether of any artistic value or not is no concern of hers, but of enough commercial value to earn a spot in a gallery, to catch the eyes of potential buyers, and to fetch at least two hundred dollars each, as compensation for Loan and her, the aggrieved parties when our contract was broken.

Tomorrow I turn thirty-nine.

Twenty years ago, fresh out of high school, I passed the entrance exams for the University of Fine Arts. Such a stupid thing to have done. As early as the day I got my results slip, I had known that it was such a stupid thing. My art education lasted five years. During those five years my parents rejoiced over my five certificates of achievement, as compensation for the five times they were summoned to the headmasters' offices of each high school where I was registered, made to repeat a year, or from which I was expelled. Those five years of university was the first contract I ever signed, and with no one else but my own parents. I was in charge of the spiritual side, my parents the material. Both sides were satisfied. On the day I presented my degree of Distinction to my parents, my mother prepared a sumptuous feast and my father poured me a glass of imported wine, both as distinguished as my grade. The memory of that day is still vivid in my mind. After the lavish lunch, I left our family apartment for good, with not a penny to my name, the degree certificate dutifully left with my parents as proof of a contract fulfilled to mutual satisfaction. I would go on to sign other contracts with strangers. Short-term and long-term. Extremely important and not so important. But never again would I be in charge of the spiritual side.

Tomorrow I turn thirty-nine.

Four years ago, Loan had a motorbike accident. Her colleague came to tell me the news and offered to take me straight to the hospital. I accepted without hesitation, as I also didn't think I'd be able to go on my own. My wife's due date was a week away. Her doctor had warned her to be cautious, especially in the final days. The journey to the hospital seemed endless. I seemed to meet challenges at every step, the streets being too crowded, the intersections too many, at every intersection a red light, at every red light a traffic policeman, the difficult old guard who didn't want to let us in because it was supposed to be the patients' rest time, the obstinate nurse who demanded to see my ID before showing me to Loan's room. But when I saw her on the bed, smiling a big smile, the world around me darkened. A disappointment like I had never experienced washed over me. Then and there I realized that I had wanted to see Loan as soon as possible because I'd been sure that she was dead. My imagination had jumped ahead and my eyes had seen her body covered in blood and shrouded in white sheets, my ears had heard the scurrying rats in the cold room, my nose had smelled formaldehyde, my brain had wondered about the exact way that substance keeps days-old phở noodles nice and fresh, a sensational news story that provoked ubiquitous wrath a while ago. But I didn't find it scary or revolting, that chemical smell of embalmment; at least, it didn't make me puke.

I woke to Loan tapping my shoulder, still wearing the same smile that had been plastered on her face for the last fifteen minutes. I still remember how I left her on her own and went looking for the head of the department. He was occupied with a special brain surgery. The patient, female like Loan, had also been involved in a motorbike accident. I stood outside the operating room, eyes glued to the glass door, as agitated as if it had been my wife inside. After thirty minutes, the grim-faced surgeons and nurses called for a break. I went to the husband and shook his hand.

His hand was limp. I asked, is it a cracked skull. He didn't seem to understand at first, but after a few seconds he buried his face in his hands and bawled. He wouldn't quiet down until a nurse came in and scolded him, she isn't dead you know. During the lunch break, the department head let me in. Leaving me standing in the middle of the room, he immediately explained, there's a deep fracture to the skull, we don't expect her to make it through the week. Ah, he thought it was my wife on the operating table. I set him straight, saying Loan was only recently admitted and hadn't even gone through imaging. He frowned and waved me away, saying the results would be in the next day. The door slammed shut. I found myself banished outside, eyes wide open, they hadn't so much as blinked since Loan woke me up. Thanks to the doctor's blank expression and ambiguous words, I felt optimistic again, even hopeful. That night I sat nodding in the hospital corridor, wishing for daybreak, wishing that the doctor would arrive at work punctually to read Loan's brain X-ray. At one point in my dream, I saw him holding up a scan, indicating a big black blob smack in the middle of the skull, making sure to point out Loan's name underneath, then turning back to give me a long meaningful look, smiling and nodding. I was still wondering how to respond to such tact when I was woken up again. Loan was tapping on my shoulder, smiling a smile even bigger than yesterday, she said the department head was too busy to come but had called to say she could be discharged right away, her skull was intact, she would go on to have her baby on the due date.

My jaw dropped. That day I forgot to brush my teeth, to eat breakfast or lunch, and didn't feel hungry even when I went to bed at ten. And since that day Loan has flashed her smile countless times, each time with a few taps on my shoulder, just to remind me, I suspect, that victory was hers, that she would never let me bail out of our contract, which the birth of our child a week later made more binding than ever before.

I suspected, moreover, that after the accident, Loan took great, even extreme caution in her eating and traveling, not for her own sake but to dissuade me from fantasizing about her sudden demise. The bike was refurbished and sold to a neighbor, at a loss of one million đồng. My wife vowed that from then until the end of her life, she would only cycle, and always hugging the curb. Sometimes, smiling and tapping my shoulder, she would announce that she'd just had her Purple Star chart read by this or that astrologer, all of whom assured her that her fate was so rock-solid that she could expect deliverance even on the brink of death by some guardian angel. I had the feeling that ultimately my wife, a woman of limited intellect, had managed to become immortal due solely to her desire to subdue me, to hold me forever accountable to that contract. Her conviction dated from as early as the day we got married. It was so strong that when she knew herself to be pregnant, Loan stated as a fact that the baby would be a girl. I couldn't understand her at the time. Only nine months later, taking our daughter from her hands, astonished to see how the baby's face was a carbon copy of her mother's, did I realize that my wife held a fanatical belief that, even in the event of her dropping dead, this baby would be her replacement in everything. Most importantly, in the contract she and I signed. From the moment she was born, my daughter knew enough to cry hysterically at the sight of her father. I clapped my hands over my ears and was about to throw her away from me when Loan tapped my shoulder, smiling that big smile, and asked if I thought it was a good idea to name the baby after her. Ah, I suspect that this, too, was not unrehearsed.

The next four years we spent together only strengthened Loan's conviction about her own immortality. I guessed this was what most fueled my disgust at our shared life. And it's why I never repent the fact that every single day during that life, I silently wished for her death. I didn't know what kind of death. I didn't know and I didn't care. All I cared about was this: she'd be gone from my life, gone forever.

Tomorrow I turn thirty-nine.

Fifty-three days ago, I got sick. At first I supposed that it was mere heat exhaustion. But when the night came, my limbs felt numbingly cold, and my teeth chattered nonstop. Then I threw up, and didn't feel better afterward, only tired to the bone. My wife made a big show of being concerned. She called some doctor to come see me in the middle of the night, and when morning came she even hired a taxi to take me to the hospital for a blood test. I was kept there for three days. After three days the doctors didn't find a thing. I lost three kilos, and my face turned haggard. My wife acted even more worried, she kept asking my doctor if I needed an X-ray, asking me what I wanted to eat, what I wanted to drink, only leaving me alone at nine when the clock announced the end of visiting hours. But Loan always came in early the next day. Those three nights turned out to be the most pleasant since my marriage. Turned out Loan's absence was enough in itself to improve my quality of life. I tried to eat little, to vomit every three hours, to produce some blood in my vomit, to make the blood darker and darker, so that I could extend my stay for a few more days. But the attempt was doomed from the start. The medical industry was suffering from a severe shortage of beds, and patients with nameless diseases like mine couldn't stay more than three days, not for love or even ready money.

Night. Night was yellow, the color of that single small bulb in the corridor.

Not a soul in the vast hospital.

I strolled around for the last time. I had strolled many laps around this yard during the last thirty-six hours. In a few hours Loan would arrive, this time to take me home. I knew she had been pulling all the strings to get me discharged ASAP. Evidently, the hospital was not a favorable setting for our contract. The door of the X-ray room was wide open, and this time again there was no one inside. A hunch told me that my files were on the desk right in the middle of the room. They were preparing for my discharge. An idea crossed my mind. I recalled the man in the room next door, around my age, whom I'd seen that afternoon bidding his wife a teary-eyed goodbye. He was due to be sent home the next day. Yes, there was his name. His files were just a few folders away from my own. In glee I pictured Loan bawling. Ah, I wondered if her guardian angels would come and save her now.

That night I slept like a log. I deliberately overslept my scheduled discharge. I only woke up at the sound of Loan shouting at the nurse, who was trying to come up with an explanation for the crack in my skull, freshly discovered on the X-ray last night and declared incurable by the specialists. I had the impression that the old guard was winking at me, and the janitor lady was waving to me when I passed through the hospital gates. With hardly a glance back, I clutched my papers in my hands.

Outside, Loan frowned when she realized I was still in my hospital clothing. I opened my duffel bag and took out my raincoat. It had been only three days, but I felt the raincoat had already doubled in size, already too long, its color already too gray. Startled, I looked at the bag. The bag itself didn't seem like my old bag anymore. I would be leaving Hà Nội in a month, but the feeling of that moment would stay with me forever.

In the taxi, all the way home from the hospital, neither of us said a word.

That very night, the divorce paper was left on her pillow, with my signature at the bottom.

Loan looked at me without saying anything. Her eyes were red. Finally, I guessed, the crack in the skull of the patient next door was what made her sign the paper. Or maybe it was the apartment, or the motorbike, or the fifty paintings I was about to paint. I didn't know, and I didn't care. All I cared about was this: when those fifty days came to an end, I would wake up in the morning and find her gone from my life, gone forever, as if we'd never met, as if the last five years had been nothing but a nightmare.

That was how I started it. I sent what I'd written to a paper. It was taken as a short story. I thought of it as a short story myself. I wanted it to end there. I knew I had to end it there if I wanted to start something else. Like wrapping up a period of one's life, ten years or twenty. Or ten months or twenty. A period of one's life all the same. Ready to be wrapped up. Or, cannot but be wrapped up. But I knew, too, that at some point in the future I would take it out and continue writing. What I'd written might be the first, or it might be the last chapter. But it can't be a short story. It can't end where I'd ended it. I knew how hard it is, the act of ending something. As hard as wrapping up a period of one's life. A period of a life cannot be a short story. Ten years or twenty cannot be a short story. And neither can ten months or twenty. I know at some point in the future I will take it out and continue writing. Continue to reach an end. Continue to wrap it up. I don't write about Thụy. I don't write to Thụy. For the last twelve years I have been wanting to see him, to ask. But I don't write to him. I didn't dare write to him. I'm afraid that I have nothing to write to him. Once again I read *The North China Lover*. Duras has nothing to write to her lover. She doesn't give his name. She doesn't remember his family name. His homeland is simply stated as Manchuria. Manchuria is the size of France. Her book is dedicated to "Thanh." *I'm Yellow* is dedicated to no one. I know Thụy's name. I know his family name. I have been to Yên Khê, where he was born three months and two days before me. On the bus, he put his head on my shoulder. He told me things. He slept. At school no one associated with him. He never dared take a day off. He trudged in even when he was sick. A day off meant a lesson lost. No classmate would share their notes with him. No one wanted to have anything to do with him. And he didn't want to go to their homes. He didn't want to face their parents. Their parents would see him and ask, hey when are you going back to your country, have you sold all your furniture yet. Before the school trip, the school managers called a meeting with the secretary of the school youth union and the teacher of ideology. Every day Chinese gunners threaten to fire five cannonballs over the China-Vietnam border. Student Âu Phương Thụy's family have expressed their wish to stay in Hà Nội. The party has not yet made up their mind. The family has not shown any signs yet. But it's our duty to ensure that he is watched closely. Put to a vote, 50 percent of staff members favored having Thụy stay at home. The other half were for letting him join the trip. Finally the ideology teacher decided, we will show Beijing who is the shrewder. Student Âu Phương Thụy would go to Yên Khê all the same. It's our duty to ensure that he is watched closely. If Beijing's cannonballs want to reach Yên Khê, they'll have to get past us first. It's our duty to ensure that he is watched closely. The next day the whole students' discipline committee was ready to watch him. The next day again all class officers were ready to watch him. By the weekend the whole student body was ready to watch him. The school security guard pledged to compose a daily three-page report about him. On the bus he told me he was born in Yên Khê. He slept with his head on my shoulder. His hair was cropped. His eyes were slanted. At sixteen, he was as tall as Vĩnh is now. Duras describes how her North China Lover smells of silk, of jade, of cigarette anglaise. Duras can never forget the fragrance of silk, of jade, of cigarette anglaise. I remember how his hair was cropped, how his eyes were slanted. After my five-year stay in Russia, I came back to find his hair still cropped, his eyes still slanted. Neither of us had anything fragrant enough to remember to this day. My Leningrad friends were the only guests at my wedding. My mother was ill. Had been ill for half a year. Ever since the day I announced my firm decision to marry Thụy. My father didn't touch his food. Didn't touch his food for a whole week. He'd always been thin but now he was bony. The house was like a house in mourning. I didn't dare look at my mother. I didn't dare look at my father. We didn't dare look at one another. If by chance we found ourselves face-to-face, our eyes automatically dropped to the ground. Thụy said his parents wanted to visit. Even skipping the traditional premarital rites, the two families should at least meet once before the wedding day. My mother said she had no mind to discuss my getting married. My mother was ill. My father was silent. At dinner, he just held his chopsticks and stared at his bowl. The rice in the bowl hadn't diminished by a single grain by the time the table was cleared. On my wedding day, the house was still like a house in mourning. I didn't dare remind my parents. We didn't dare look at one another. Neither my father nor my mother mentioned Thụy even once. In the twenty-three years we were together. My parents kept acting as if there was no Thụy. His very name was boycotted. Along with the whole of China. From tofu pudding to Kong Fu Zi, Lao Zi. From wonton noodles to Mao Ze Dong, Deng Xiao Ping. From luk dau sa soup to Sun Wu Kong, Zhu Ba Jie. I've never met anyone whose Sinophobia was as perfect as my parents'. From A to Z. Categorically. No compromise. No mitigating circumstances. No exceptional pardon. From A to Z. Last year my father sent me a copy of his family tree. Early this year my mother sent me a copy of hers. Both experts from the Institute of History failed to locate any Chinese ancestor in either my father's or my mother's lines. But those experts could only go back ten generations. Who can say for sure that his or her eleventh forefather was true-blooded Vietnamese. I imagine that someday, some cousin once or twice removed will take it upon himself to reconstruct our family history, and after countless visits to the National Library of Vietnam, the National Archive, the École Française d'Extrême-Orient, and the Institut des Civilisations Orientales in Paris, will find that only five generations back there was this Âu, tired of a life mixing medicinal herbs, who packed up and rowed southward until settling in Yuenan, and not because the grass there was greener but because it was where the Red River came to an end, and no amount of effort could turn boat and oars into chariot and horses. Therefore, he had to stay. Therefore my father, five generations later. I imagine further that someday my mother's expert from the Institute of History will be denounced in some conference by an expert from the Institute of Sino-Nôm Studies, as relying not upon scientific proof but on hearsay and anecdote, even old wives' tales. This Sino-Nôm expert, as well-versed in Old Chinese as he is in Old Vietnamese, will advocate a new approach based on tombstone inscriptions, which yields resounding evidence that, five generations back, there was this batman of a Chinese mandarin who fled the court when it came to light that he had accepted a bribe. The disgraced mandarin built a ship and sailed to the Indonesian Sea intending to go to Australia and then Europe, but ran ashore in Yuenan after many a day battling storms and piracy. After ten years of devoted service to his master, whom no one now knew had once served the Northern emperor, the batman was rewarded with the hand of a local mulberry-picking girl. The couple raised silkworms for a living and gave birth to five sons, all with the family name Âu, all with cropped hair and slanted eyes. The five sons in their turn married five local mulberry girls, raised silkworms, and gave birth to five sons each. The twenty-five sons married twenty-five local mulberry girls, raised silkworms, and gave birth to five sons each. One of them adopted a Vietnamese family name at eighteen, the tombstone fails to say why, but still married a local mulberry girl, and this couple too raised silkworms and gave birth to five sons, the youngest of whom was my mother's father, who still retained his cropped hair and slanted eyes, the spitting image of the other six hundred and twenty-four descendants of the batman of yore, only minus the Âu name. I imagine how my parents would react to the news that the blood in their veins is partly Chinese. My father would surely stop touching his food. My mother would surely fall ill. Their house would be like a house in mourning. My father would demand that the cousin be sued. My mother would demand to speak to the expert's superior. My parents would bar their door to our relatives, who are only too eager to be introduced to Thụy's mother, now the incumbent Hà Nội brand representative of Tai Feng limited joint stock, and to Thụy himself, a means to reach Âu businessmen all over the globe. My parents would declare war on the entirety of Hà Nội's market, where every day Hà Nội consumers are made to purchase fifty thousand Chinese apples, five thousand Chinese snakehead fish, five hundred kilograms of Chinese grapes, fifty baskets of Chinese eggs, five trucks of toilet paper and diapers for babies and sanitary pads for women and condoms for men, all Chinese in origin. My parents are perfect Sinophobes. From A to Z. My parents are perfect in everything they do. Everything was done from A to Z. They portioned out my love perfectly equally among all the school subjects, my mother's love equally into glasses of sweet catjang soup, my father's love equally into steamed pig brains. During my ten years at school, I came to understand that the glasses of catjang my mother bothered to make herself were not a reward for my ten in math but to guarantee that I would bring home another ten, in physics, PE, or anything else. That was why my mother's soup needed no ice, pomelo blossoms, or shredded coconut. Its only duty was to provide me with as many calories as possible. Even now I can still taste it, that brackish, off-sweet taste of government-store candies, that overcooked bean pulp, which I always had to eat hot, even in sweltering Hà Nội summers. During my ten years at school, I came to understand that the pig brains for which my father lined up from morning till afternoon were not a reward for my ten in literature, but to guarantee that I would bring home another ten, in history or military exercises. That was why his pig brains needed no dill, pepper, or MSG, and no attempt to enliven its presentation. Even now I can still see them, aluminum bowls in the steaming rice pot, and taste the metallic tang of blood which no amount of salt could mask, and which I always had to down in one gulp. I didn't care for steamed pig brains, I had no disease to be cured by them, but every other day I closed my eyes and my nostrils and downed them in one gulp, because they were most nutritious, especially for the brain, and most of all for a child's. It was my duty to turn catjang soup and steamed pig brains into tens and praise in my school reports: outstanding, hard-working, good attendance, serious, a brilliant future awaits. "A brilliant future awaits" was music to my parents' ears. "A brilliant future awaits" gave them strength to pursue their parental duties of cooking catjang soup and lining up for pig brains. Thus was the cycle of solicitude completed. Thus were the three of us glued together by the word "duty." My parents could hardly wait until the annual parent-teacher conference, which each attended equipped with a notebook, my father to see teachers of natural sciences, my mother those of social sciences. PE, domestic science, music, art, and grenade throwing are hard to categorize, so those teachers were taken care of by both. My parents always took up an hour of the homeroom teacher's time. In the first half hour my father discussed boy students and my mother discussed girls. In the last half hour both my parents petitioned for me to be seated in the top row, in the very middle of the class. My father explained that that way I would be seen by the teachers from every direction. My mother explained that that way I wouldn't have my hand touched, my foot stepped on, my ear whispered into, my neck ruler-poked, or my exam paper copied from, by any students of either gender. During my ten years at school, I always sat alone. During my ten years at school, all I knew was the way between home to school. When classes were over, I went back home just to sit down again at my other desk and open my books. During recess, I stood in a corner and reviewed lessons for the next classes. When I'd finished, I reviewed lessons for the next day. Or the next day again. I never learned how to skip rope, how to play capture the mandarin, or chess card, or racing horses, or dominoes. In my parents' educational book, those are useless things. Salted apricots, pickled apples, candies dipped in flour, all useless. Cartoons, comic books, zoos, all useless. Birthday parties, Midautumn fests, gatherings at the end of the school year, all useless. If it wouldn't lead to tens and praise in my school reports, "useless" was the only epithet my parents found applicable. During my ten years at school, I wasn't permitted to mix with students who got "average" in marks or in conduct, who repeated a year, or who behaved badly. They, too, were useless. Thụy did not repeat a year, nor did he behave badly, but he was a "problem" student. Being a problem is even worse than repeating a year or behaving badly. Being a problem is not only useless but actively harmful. Being a problem closes all the doors leading to that brilliant future. Being a "problem" would never get into my parents' good books. My parents wouldn't let the future be marred by even the merest mosquito. My future belonged to my parents. My tens belonged to my parents. The praise in my school reports belonged to my parents. My summons to continue my studies overseas belonged to my parents. My parents didn't need to go to the award ceremony, they could stay home and indulge in the vision of me accepting the award, the headmaster praising me in front of the whole school, everyone standing up and clapping for me, the vice-headmistress presenting me with a bouquet, a box of chalks, two luxury "Deer" notebooks, then the certificate of merit from the municipal department of education, then one from the national ministry, then the whole school standing up and clapping once again. My parents didn't need to go to Russia. They could stay home and savor the image of me living my Russian life as an undergraduate, the immense lecture hall, the professor in suit and tie, his black leather briefcase and his black car, the library overflowing with books, the laboratory as large as a minifactory, the volleyball court as big as the Hàng Đẫy stadium, then the certificate of merit from the college, then one from the embassy. At the market, everyone would come to my mother to ask after the girl in the USSR. At his office, time and again a colleague would glide up to my father and inquire about the current situation there. At conferences, business trips, parties, weddings, death anniversaries, Tết, they wouldn't even need to open their mouths to advertise the fact that their only daughter was studying in the USSR, because there would always be someone eager to do it on their behalf. Later, to inform others that the same only daughter is in France doing a postgraduate. I imagine my parents raising some fancy lapdogs, selling them in the puppy market in Lạng Sơn for two thousand dollars, buying two Vietnam Airlines tickets to Paris and discovering how the Belleville apartment where I and Vĩnh are staying is just one corridor roomier than the eighteen-square-meter apartment in the Đê La Thành blocks, how my dissertation is now long abandoned, my advisor long shamefacedly avoided, how I spend three hours a day on public transport to teach a clutch of pupils who detest the word "future," detest the Ministry of Education, and detest my English lessons most of all. I don't know whether my parents know about those things, but I know they have a special talent for pretending not to know. My parents pretended not to know that Thụy's name and mine sat side by side on the covers of my tenth-grade notebooks. That his was the only visage that I cherished, that I turned toward, in my five Russian years. That the two of us met every Saturday night at the end of my street. When I went out with my friends, I would come back at ten to find my parents waiting with the lights on. My father would carry my bicycle upstairs. My mother would make me lemonade. By that time, lemonade had displaced sweet cat-jang soup, perhaps because as a government worker I needed fewer calories than in my school days, now that the tens and praise in school reports were but distant memories. When I went out with my friends, I would come back at ten to find my parents waiting with the door open. My father would ask what that girl or boy majored in, if they also had a red diploma, if they were about to go back for predoctoral studies. My mother would ask what kind of family that girl or boy came from, which ministry or university they were now working for. When I went out with Thụy, whether I came back at nine, ten, eleven, I would open the door and carry my bicycle inside to find my parents already in bed, the lights already off. My father in one bed. My mother in another. Two mosquito nets. Two backs turned. And remained turned until morning. My parents never so much as alluded to Thụy. They would never waste a thought on some "problem" person. They would never let the future be marred by even the merest mosquito. The word "future" had never needed a possessive pronoun or qualifying noun, it had belonged to all three of us since the day I was born. A week before my wedding day, I trekked back and forth across Hà Nội and managed to procure two packs of candied lotus seeds, two packets of loose Thái Nguyên tea, twenty betel leaves, and a bunch of areca nuts. I told my parents that these were from Thụy. My parents said nothing. They didn't send the gifts out to announce the marriage. I wasn't surprised by their reaction. I put everything on our ancestral altar. When the day came, the tea had grown moldy, the lotus seeds watery, the leaves darkened, the nuts as dry as wood. I packed them one by one into a plastic bag. Then put it all in the bin before leaving the house. My parents didn't come to our wedding. Neither did Thụy's. At five p.m. I went to the end of my street, where we had our rendezvous every Saturday night. Thụy was already waiting for me. Side by side we cycled to the wedding hall. He wore a white shirt and black pants. I wore a white áo dài and white pants. None of my colleagues knew that I was getting married. None of my relatives on either side. And none of my neighbors. I wasn't surprised by my parents' reaction. Neither was I surprised by their reaction when they met the guy. They heaped upon him all the affection that should have gone to Thụy. They accepted him from the first time he brought my letter to their house. My mother made him lemonade. My father carried his bicycle upstairs. I don't know in what fashion, in what language, my parents have come to know his life story as thoroughly as the palms of their hands. His line of work, his homelife, his Paul and Arthur, his parents in Rennes.

Never once have my parents let Thụy's name pass their lips. But the guy's full name, so long and difficult, they write as easily as their own. Their letters to me are in part asking after Vĩnh, in part asking after my master's degree, but mostly discussing the guy, describing his visits, always ending by asking when he and I will get married, when he and I will go back to Vietnam to do the rounds of our relatives. For the last ten years my parents have been dreaming about my wedding to the guy. A bilingual invitation, complete with my parents' names, his parents' names, my name, his name, the One Pillar Pagoda and the Eiffel Tower side by side. The bride in white áo dài, white pants, and white veil, the groom in black suit and black tie. The groom's party arriving at the bride's house in a white car, a snow-white teddy bear perched on the bonnet. Young ladies carrying trays of offerings in front, children following in droves. The groom's parents bobbing up and down in front of the altar, the bride and groom bobbing up and down in front of the altar, my parents to the side murmuring prayers. The language barrier is no problem. I am your son-in-law or I am your sonny-lewd is no problem. One shouldn't get hung up on details. Even if his parents talk west when mine talk east, this wouldn't take away from the main point, which is that the whole neighborhood and all the relatives would witness us linking arms for the flashing cameras. Nowadays Hà Nội has loads of choices when it comes to restaurants. If you two so wish, we can even book a dinner cruise on the West Lake, or the iconic Water Pavilion, or the buffet-and-banquet option in Daewoo hotel, and that Franco-Vietnamese Hoa Sữa restaurant would work all night to build your three-and-a-half-tier wedding cake, delivered on its own three-wheeled cyclo with the figurines fixed on top at the venue. The bride figurine in white áo dài and veil, the groom figurine in black suit and tie. Since I don't know when, my parents have taken to referring to me and the guy as "you two" and his parents as "his dear parents." Are his dear parents well. Send our regards to his dear parents. Father would like to send his dear father half a kilo of Trung Nguyên coffee. Mother would love to give his dear mother half a kilo of candied lotus seeds, from Hàng Điếu street no less. Since I don't know when, my parents have begun to plan our shared life, his and mine. I suspect that since the first time they set eyes on him they began to devise a future for us, which from that moment on meant the four of us. You two both left a marriage behind, that's alright, that's all the better, you can better understand each other, one shouldn't get hung up on details. You two had better make it official, move in together, it won't be a family without husband and wife, children won't be happy without mom and dad. My parents' dreams, my parents' plans, always make my stomach turn. My stomach turns when I imagine my mother making the guy lemonade, my father carrying his bicycle upstairs, and on every occasion, meeting, party, wedding, death anniversary, Tết, there is always someone eager to broadcast that my parents' only daughter is about to get a husband in France. My stomach turns so badly I don't dare imagine further. The first time he brought me a letter from them, I got up, found a pair of scissors, cut my parents' plans and dreams in half, and dumped them into the wastebasket. He didn't dare look at me. He went home bewildered. But the next time, he got it. He gave me their letter with one hand, the scissors with the other. We exchanged an amused smile. I thought he was not so bad. This time I didn't cut the letter in half. Instead, I put it into a drawer. After his eleven trips from north to south on his Soviet motorbike, I had eleven unopened letters in my drawer, filled with my parents' plans and dreams, their urge for us to get married. I imagine a scenario in which it isn't the guy but someone with the family name of Âu or Nguyễn, a waiter for some restaurant in the 13th arrondissement, who takes my letter to my parents with him in a trip to the homeland, to finally see the Turtle Tower in Hà Nội. That Âu or Nguyễn so-and-so could be younger than the guy, with a fuller head of hair, a less bulging stomach, a dexterity with chopsticks, and a real appreciation of fish sauce, but never would that Âu or Nguyễn so-and-so get my father to carry his bicycle upstairs, my mother to make him lemonade, my parents to call us "you two" or ask after his dear parents. Never would there be a wedding with the bride in a white áo dài and veil and the groom in black suit and tie, even if that Âu or Nguyễn so-and-so looked born to wear said items without needing a hem fixed or a leg altered. Never would that Âu or Nguyễn so-and-so's parents be seen bobbing up and down in front of the altar, with the bride and groom bobbing up and down in front of the altar, and my parents to the side murmuring prayers, not even if that Âu or Nguyễn so-and-so's parents could bob all day without their knees complaining if this had been my parents' wish. But this wasn't my parents' wish. This is not about their wish. My parents wouldn't let the future be marred by even the merest mosquito. My parents would never accept someone who waits tables in a capitalist country, the same way they had once denounced a "problem" person in a socialist one. This is not about politics. My parents who only yesterday extolled Russia as their paradise are today chanting to-see-Paris-and-die. Even if tomorrow nuclear-toting Putin demands to be made the lord of the Élysée, and Chirac is only too eager to be shot of his obstinate Frenchmen and assume the Kreml' throne, my parents will clap their support for both. This is not about politics. My parents don't give a damn about politics, about how to tell capitalism from socialism, or if Putin and Chirac are even the same guy. The only damn they give is about the word "future." In the 1980s that word was brilliantly colored with the red of Soviet Russia. A daughter with a Russian degree, a son-in-law also with a Russian degree, coming home for a placement in this ministry or that university. After a few years, daughter and son-in-law would again study for the subdoctorate entrance exams, and my father would be more than happy to line up for two pig brains a day, my mother to unwrap some more government-store candies for two glasses of sweet catjang soup. While we wait to defend our theses in Russia, we should use the time to join the party, wouldn't "Subdoctorate" look so nice followed by "Party member" on our visiting cards, and we mustn't forget to buy a refrigerator and a TV set so as to have something to fill our overseas crates, not to mention some dozens of pressure cookers, and hundreds of wheel bearings to act as cushioning for the tottering goods during the three-month voyage. If there's still time, why don't we go on to have a baby boy, an early taste for butter and milk and a smattering of babbled Russian will mean he won't seem such a bumpkin when he comes back at eighteen in his turn. When our own studies are over and we're back in Vietnam, it's best we free some space by selling all those cookers and stuff, and buy a Soviet-designed prefab apartment in Kim Liên blocks, somewhere to display the Soviet fridge and Soviet TV set. A few more years and we can apply for doctorate courses, my father won't be too old to line up for pig brains, nor my mother too feeble to make catjang soup. While we wait to defend our doctoral theses in Russia, we'll do well to soothe the pain of the uprooted by getting to know our brothers in the embassy and trade office. We mustn't be difficult if the embassy brothers want us to pull our weight by shouldering the party secretaryship at our PhD institution. We mustn't be reluctant if the trade office brothers need us to do them a favor by filling containers of knitting machines with dozens of fridges and TVs, since the shipping fee from the Port of Odessa to the Port of Hải Phòng has already be paid in full by the Nam Định textile factory. On our third time coming back to Vietnam, we two will be approaching forty, with visiting cards indicating both doctorate and party membership, brilliantly red letters for both Russian and Vietnamese. Wife as faculty head and husband as research department head, or vice versa, one shouldn't get hung up on details after all. Several times a year we'll attend parties at Hà Nội's Soviet embassy, mingling and fraternizing with Soviet experts, or go back for conferences in the very land of the Soviets, reuniting with our embassy and trade office brothers in Moskva, in which case we mustn't miss the opportunity to bring them our ever so popular T-shirts with the ochna prints, our eye-liners or our color-changing sunglasses, so that the two flimsy sheets with our typed-up research proposals will have some company traveling in the cardboard boxes. We shouldn't take our rubles back to Vietnam, in case the USSR suddenly ups and changes its currency. They should be sent to whatever brothers are there on postgrad fellowships, they have plenty of time on their hands, they can line up to buy antibiotics on our behalf, a few thousand blister packs to bring back for our ten million fellow citizens, who use Soviet antibiotics for everything under the sun. And with all this back and forth, we'll never risk forgetting the six cases of Russian nouns. Our children will easily understand the odd khorosho we'll drop in conversation, as they'll be enrolled at seven years old in Hà Nội's most intensive Russian classes, plus our friends will all be red-diploma khorosho folks who are eyeing this institute's vice-presidency or that university's directorship, and from whose pockets a stack of brilliant red Doctor-and-Party-member name cards are too prone to falling out. As brilliant as the red my parents use to color the word "future." The word "future" came crashing down the day the USSR dissolved, when Vietnamese students and postgrads in Russia couldn't even find any cabbage to cook with mutton. My parents shed a single tear over the socialist bloc, but soaked two handkerchiefs between them over the word "future." For a whole week my mother was ill in bed, my father wouldn't touch his food, the house was like a house in mourning. On the eighth day, my parents roused themselves. My parents are not the resigning type. They wrung out both handkerchiefs and resolved to find a new promised land to sow with the F word. Every cloud has a silver lining, the truth of which was proven after just a few months. Having washed off the brilliant red coat of donated Soviet paint and donned the new cloak of perestroikaesque đổi mới, my country suddenly found itself extraordinarily attractive to strangers. With tentative steps, Western Europe drew near. Its interest was piqued by the exotic scents. France was first to stretch out a gallant hand, having the advantage of past ties, strained and gnawed at but not completely severed, the Indochinese scents after all those years having lost none of their Indochinese allure. The early 1990s saw an exodus of Vietnamese surging toward Paris, with the true Francophone folks in the vanguard, two hundred elderly grandpas and grandmas who'd sampled the vin, the fromage, the toi et moi in the first quarter of their lives. Behind them came two hundred teachers and students of whatever French departments remained, who were still learning how to enjoy the vin, the fromage, the toi et moi from their textbooks. Bringing up the rear were those who knew nothing of the vin, the fromage, the toi et moi, but in just a few years had become a force to be reckoned with, thanks to their commendable flexibility, formed facing hardships unparalleled in Vietnam's contemporary history. Amid this last rank my parents could be glimpsed. I still remember like it was yesterday, a night toward the end of the year when my father rushed into my eighteen-square-meter apartment in Đê La Thành blocks. My mother rushed in behind him. My father got a xeroxed sheet from his briefcase. My mother took it and handed it to me. My father lowered his voice and said, we have something for you. My mother lowered her voice and repeated, we have something for you. My parents' talent for voice-lowering never ceases to amaze me. I said I was in no mind to think about exams. My father rose abruptly. My mother rose abruptly. I said it had only been half a year since Thụy left. My father pretended not to hear me. My mother also pretended not to hear me. I said Vĩnh was just a baby. My father burst into tears. My mother also burst into tears. For a week my father didn't touch his food. For a week my mother was ill in bed. The house was like a house in mourning. I didn't touch my food. And Vĩnh was ill in bed. I lay hugging him all day. The week finally passed. My parents wrung out their two handkerchiefs. They opened my wardrobe. My father put all of my clothes into a bag. My mother put all of Vĩnh's into another. Thụy's lay untouched. I put a scarf around my neck and a wool hat on Vĩnh's head. My father went out first. My mother followed. I was last with my baby. I didn't turn back for a final look at the apartment. And I didn't say goodbye to my neighbors. Silently we marched toward the word "future." The word "future" was also flexible in the era of đổi mới. The word "future" suggested that my parents let go of catjang soup and pig brains and take up care of baby Vĩnh. The word "future" commanded me to win first place in the graduate school exams at the French embassy, held to celebrate the normalization of bilateral relations. I went through three pairs of eyeglasses, three language centers, three tutors, and three sets of books, but when my parents rushed to the results board they didn't find me in the first, second, or even third place. They were on the point of calling an ambulance to Việt Đức's cardiac department when they finally found my name, at the very bottom. In the era of đổi mới even my parents became flexible. They no longer took valedictorianship to be the only measure of honor. They were content enough to color the word "future" with red, white, and blue. Its Soviet hue had faded in less than a year. My parents don't need to go to France themselves. My father only needs to lie on his bed at nine p.m. and picture the Air France plane soaring westward with me in it. My mother says food and drink are vanity of vanities. It's enough that I can enjoy on her behalf the vin, the fromage, the toi et moi. My parents ask anyone who is going to France to bring me a half kilo of Trung Nguyên coffee and the same of Hàng Điếu lotus seeds, gifts for the guy's dear parents. But the half kilo of candied lotus seeds I bought for my wedding day was left to grow soggy on the altar. Since they first set eyes on the guy, my parents had been busily planning a Franco-Vietnamese wedding. But my Sino-Vietnamese wedding that actually took place, they opted not to attend. Neither did Thụy's parents. The day went by in a flurry. The only guests were my few friends from Leningrad. They came with their children. Their children born in the USSR, who'd had just a taste of butter and milk before boarding the plane to the homeland. The wedding was their first time meeting Thụy. They asked me in Russian, so this is your architect beau. He didn't understand. He just smiled awkwardly. He stood there embarrassed. Then they asked him, in Vietnamese, where are you working, which office, which department. This time he was even more embarrassed. His smile grew fixed. I intervened, saying he was "between offices." I changed the subject. Changing the subject was my forte. I came to master it during my time dating Thụy. Who's that boy I saw you with on Bà Triệu street yesterday. Last week I called and called and you were so absorbed in talking to whoever-it-is. Look at you two lost in that movie, I guess the invites will be sent out soon, eh. I always changed the subject. After five years of my changing the subject, people were used to it and left me alone. My friends weren't used to it, but they made no comment. I talked about the old days. I tried to recall funny anecdotes. In a kids' wedding, any junk could pass for food. Every bride was due soon. So were most of the female guests. Dormitories for students in the fourth year and above were virtual nurseries. Kid parents caring for their actual kids. No space in their heads for anything other than diapers and cloths, baby food and formulas. Actively aiming for bad marks so they could repeat another year, could stay on another year, even if there was no more scholarship there was always cabbage, your tongue wouldn't blister even after a whole year of cabbage. A day not having to go home is a day gained. They all burst out laughing. They told me I had such a stubborn memory. They themselves had forgotten it all. They forgot it all the moment they touched down at Nội Bài airport. Their own babies took a month to forget the taste of milk and butter. You should forget in order to live, they told me. It's the truth. Forget in order to live. They said I was the only one who'd worked hard, taking notes for everyone in class by day and writing letters to Vietnam by night. They cast meaningful glances in Thụy's direction. They clamored for the bride and groom to kiss. Kiss, like Soviet lovers do. Come kiss! Come do a Soviet! I looked at Thụy, flustered. He looked at me, flustered. We had never kissed in front of other people. In the twenty or so times we had kissed, we'd never managed to land on the lips in the first attempt. Again my friends clamored. No way would they let us off the hook without a kiss. I tugged at Thụy's sleeve. His face was crimson. I tugged at him again. Flustered, he embraced me. I pressed my lips onto his. It was the first time I didn't hit his chin or nose. Around us they clapped like thunder. Thụy's face was crimson. But they weren't done yet. Kiss again. Do a Soviet again. I tugged at his sleeve. Flustered, he embraced me. I pressed my lips onto his. Upper on upper, lower on lower. Around us they clapped like thunder. The wedding finally became sort of merry. We kissed more in those two hours than we had in the previous two years. I told myself it was good my friends were there. And good my parents weren't. With my parents around, my friends would have been too timid for such antics. With my parents around, Thụy would have been too timid to touch me, and I him. We would have exchanged solemn looks. My parents would have exchanged solemn looks. My friends' children too would have exchanged solemn looks. At nine p.m., the old guard came in and said, time's up. My friends stayed behind to help me clean. We swept the watermelon seeds, washed the teacups, took down the backdrop made of red cloth and appliquéd with our cursive, interlocked initials. Thụy made it himself. He was the one who bought the cloth, cut out the characters, glued them on. He also cut out a graceful Chinese "fú," meaning

Fortune. The first time his Chinese was put to use. I hadn't known he had done it. We hadn't even mentioned decorations. We had only wanted the wedding to be the least fuss possible. I had bought some gerberas and arranged them myself. The flowers were divided among the children when the wedding was over. The vases were returned to the wedding hall. The old guard got a packet of peanut brittle as thanks. My friends looked at me and Thụy with concern. Poor thing, they said, all you know is study, look at your myopic eyes, they will soon run out of glasses for you. Life is hard, they said, you can't be as carefree as in the old days. You must forget in order to live. It's the truth. Forget in order to live. That was the same thing I heard when I was pregnant with Vĩnh. That was what greeted me when I took the baby home. Thụy left after a month, and I heard it again in so many words. People warned me that life is thorny and my feet uncalloused. At nine thirty p.m., Thụy and I cycled home from the wedding hall. We didn't say a word. He didn't suggest it and neither did I, but when we neared the blocks, our two bicycles both turned toward the Red River. We got to a secluded spot on the sandbank, where we used to spend our Saturday nights. The river was not wide enough. The water was not clear enough. Thụy and I were both silent. I had already forgotten about our wedding just an hour before. I had forgotten that we had kissed, for the first time in front of people, for the first time our lips meeting right where they should. I thought of my parents, of our shared life drawn out until just now. Only now did I feel like not having to live for them, to think of them whatever I did, wherever I went, to fear even when kissing Thụy of offending them, offending the life shared by the three of us, marring the future belonging to all three of us. Only at twenty-seven could I set aside my love for my parents. Was that already too late. I could have done it a long long time ago. A month, a year, or three years, four years. Only at twenty-seven did I start to live for myself. Was that already too late. When

I had done getting that red diploma for my parents' sake, I should have come back to a new place of my own, made my own lemonade, carried my own bicycle upstairs to stash by the end of my own bed, with two chain locks to secure the wheels. Later, lying beside Vĩnh in our Belleville apartment, again I told myself I should not have let my mother cook me the new mother's diet of daily porridge with pig's trotter and banana blossom, to feed to me spoon by spoon because Vĩnh kept spitting his rubber nipple to the ground. I should not have let my father go to the public water tap every morning carrying a basinful of gauze diapers, and wash, and hang, and iron, and fold, and make some milk for me and Vĩnh, and carry our bathwater upstairs in pails, and fan us until we fell asleep, and swat the mosquitoes biting us both. When Vĩnh was three months old, I went back to work. Every day my parents took him to the nursery, and took him home, and prepared him some porridge, then flour soup, then rice. They were there when he caught chicken pox or whooping cough. They were there when he got a tummy bug or impetigo. Vĩnh's maternal grandparents were the ones who bathed him in bitter melon infusion to help with his rash, who made him minced pork porridge when a sore throat troubled him, who dressed him in colorful clothing for the Midautumn festival, who bounced him around on a bicycle every Sunday, who took him to peach blossom markets shopping for Tết. I don't know how great a part calculation for my future, or our three-way future, or simply the future, with no qualifying noun or possessive pronoun, played in their devotion to Vĩnh. Neither of them ever mentioned the Thống Nhất, evoked Thụy's name, voiced blame or complaints. As if there was no Thụy on earth, as if there had never been any Thụy in our three-way shared life. My parents have a special talent for pretending not to know. My parents have a special talent for rationalism. My father and my mother are one and the same. From their everyday pleasures (boiled kohlrabi for dinner) to their ambitions (first the Soviet red diploma, then the French postgraduate thesis). From their familial relations (both in awe of my mother's younger brother and his wife) to their social relations (both hostile to the Chinese). From their past (they are a twenty-five-year updated version of my paternal and maternal grandparents) to their future (me). From their jar of toothpicks to their bottle of fish sauce. From their chamber pot to their parallel snoring. My father and mother are one and the same, the same even in their ability never to go near the other's bed. Even when a relative from the countryside stays overnight, my parents stick firmly to their respective beds. The men would rub their feet together, clear their throat loudly and climb onto my father's bed. The women would rub their feet together, clear their throat and climb onto our bed, to lie squarely between my mother and me. Even when I came down with something contagious and the doctor forbade anyone to share my bed, my parents stayed steadfast in not joining their pillows and sheets. One night my father slept on the floor and I on his bed. The next night my mother slept on the floor and I on hers. Both suffered from a sore throat until it was announced on the television that the disease had left Hà Nội for the southern provinces. On Teachers' Day, on Gregorian New Year, on Tết, on Women's Day, on Labor Day, I tagged along when they visited my homeroom teacher and the teachers of all my other classes, even PE and domestic science, of course. My term-end exam result in literature topped the class without any re-marking, and my math GPA needed no half-point manipulation to catapult me from Good to Distinction. My grades were distinguished on their own, no thanks to my parents' visits. My parents didn't love or admire my teachers any more than they did their superiors. But they kept up with the visits all the same. The same way they kept sitting, fifteen minutes every year, in the living rooms of their directors and vice-directors, department heads and vice-heads. My parents didn't love or admire these people any more than they did my teachers. But those were relationships in need of constant cultivation. A matter of principle, as my parents were fond of saying. The same way they kept on diligently taking a bunch of bananas and a duck to my uncle and aunt's. My uncle and aunt didn't need the bananas and the ducks. At the sight of the bananas, my aunt would wave them away. Every day my aunt received fifty bunches of bananas from fifty caretakers of patients in the Vietnam-Cuba hospital. My aunt would turn them into sweet banana soup, banana pastries, stir-fried banana with snails and tofu, banana with eel stew, and yet there remained forty-nine bunches to be laboriously bagged, then laboriously carried to Bắc Qua market for consignment at a fruit stand. At the sight of the duck, my uncle would wave it away. Every week without fail the food company for which my uncle was political officer would send over a dozen ducks too substandard for them to sell in good conscience. My aunt would butcher and pluck the dozen substandard ducks, turning them into fried duck, roasted duck, boiled duck, duck braised with lotus seeds. My twin cousins would scream bloody murder at the smell of duck, so five butchered and plucked ducks had to be consigned at the duck-porridge inn at the end of the street. At ten the twins were already diagnosed with a surplus of duck fat in their blood. My parents were present at the Vietnam-Cuba hospital when the doctors, underlings of my aunt, stuck four syringes into their bellies and withdrew four 75cc bottles' worth of duck fat. But still my parents diligently visited my uncle and aunt, so that the next day my aunt's sack would groan under the weight of yet another bunch of bananas, and the unsuspecting porridge inn patrons ordering their second serving of substandard duck would again be duped to think it was duck sold in the very Duck Street. It was a matter of principle, my parents said, those relationships needed constant cultivation. My parents, they strived to cultivate so many relationships, yet were so completely neglectful of their own marital one. Never did I hear my father slap my mother's buttocks and her retort by calling him an old goat. Never did I see my mother's face grow sullen on nights when the power was cut or any breezeless summer noon when my father's gaze got hooked on the carelessly displayed thighs of a lady next door. Never was I jolted awake by some midnight gasps to get a glimpse of my mother quivering under my father's forty-five kilograms, of the bed quaking under their combined weight of exactly ninety kilograms. Never, not even once, since my ears could hear and my eyes could see, did my eyes and ears witness my parents cultivating their marital relationship. Luckily this was Vietnam, so this negligence didn't lead them to court, our room for three being divided with woven bamboo screens, me having breakfast with mother, dinner with father, and home from school taking half a cup of rice from his barrel and half from hers to cook and eat on my own at twelve p.m. every day. I couldn't tell if their parents being overly diligent in cultivating their marital relationship was the reason why, unlike me, my friends never got top grades in every single subject, or why, unlike me, they never received praise in their school reports like "hard-working" and "outstanding" and "brilliant future awaits." I couldn't tell if it was me and our shared three-way future that distracted my parents away from the slaps on the thighs, the squeezes of the buttocks, the pinches and pokes, the fits, though always unconscious, of jealousy. Thụy and I sat on the bank. The river was not wide enough. The water was not clear enough. Later, reading other, any other authors' works, I tell myself I can never write sex the way they do. Sexual fantasies are even more impossible. My pen freezes each time it touches upon sex. One hour after our wedding had finished, Thụy and I sat on the bank. The river was not wide enough. The water was not clear enough. I was not brave enough to kiss Thụy, my hands and lips freezing the same way they would ten years later whenever I think about writing sex. Ten years later, I still remember that that night on our new bed, we didn't pounce upon one another, or devour one another, or drain one another of energy, or shower on one another all the words of adulation, the way authors never tire of describing. Not until twenty-seven did I leave my mother's bed and Thụy leave his father's. Was it already too late. My pupils, a bunch of teenagers, spend whole classes yawning and discussing steamy movies. They say steamy movies shown on television are frightfully outdated, and French television itself is also frightfully outdated to show steamy movies with barely a wisp of steam, to rub their noses in the pathetic positions practiced by their grandparents. They mime wildly with their arms and legs. They shriek with laughter. In their dreams they never see sweet catjang soup replete with shredded coconut and pomelo blossom oil. In their dreams what they see must be fulfilling both gastrically and visually. McDonald's burgers are not enough. At thirteen, they munch on McDonald's burgers while watching steamy movies. I start talking and they toot, they hoot, they reprimand me for not knowing better, to keep my mouth shut and listen to their lecture on steamy movies. I give them a test and immediately they protest. I have no right to give a test when the lesson isn't over, they argue. They threaten to report me to the vice-headmaster and headmaster. I put on a tape and immediately they protest. They can listen until their ears wear out and they would never speak as well as the tape, they argue. I myself cannot speak as well as the tape. I myself speak with a Soviet accent. They threaten to report me to the vice-headmaster and headmaster. I put on a video tape and immediately they protest. I haven't planned the lesson so I seek to kill time, they argue. They threaten to report me to the vice-headmaster and headmaster. I read them a dictation and immediately they protest. I know nothing of pedagogy, they argue. All that I know is the old Vietnamese pedagogical methods. They threaten to report me to the vice-headmaster and headmaster. I make illustrations, I xerox materials not found in textbooks, I cut and paste, I try my best at decidedly non-Vietnamese pedagogical techniques, and immediately they protest. At any rate they don't stand a chance of getting into England or America, they argue. No one will let them into England or America. They themselves don't give a damn about getting into England or America. They can just drop ten euros and see some steamy movies right here, which have steam enough for their needs. They are bored stiff with my class. My class is worse than useless. My class is even more pathetic than their grandparents' positions. English or Americanish is worse than useless. English or Americanish is even more pathetic than steamy movies shown on French television. The vice-headmaster winks at me as he passes by my classroom: kids these days, eh. The headmaster seeks me out and shakes my hand: hang in there do your best. Everyone is so friendly. Everyone is so sympathetic. The most friendly and sympathetic are my fellow English teachers, who promptly handed me the problem classes of all three years, with the highest number of worst-behaved pupils and lowest GPAs, with parents who come to meet teachers in their nightwear. Every year I would start at a new school. In every school they would promptly hand me their three problem classes. In every school my fellow English teachers would say that burdens are to be shared, someone else shouldered it last year so now it's my turn, and someone else will take it over from me next year. But come next year I would have started at a new school again. They would also say that a new school every year trumps a new school every three, four, or five months. Three months subbing for a male colleague on sick leave. Four months subbing for a female colleague on maternity leave. Five months subbing for a colleague, no one knows their gender, who is neither sick nor on maternity leave but went AWOL after the first day of school, the Ministry of Education is circulating their photo ID everywhere to ascertain their whereabouts. When each year draws to an end I tell myself again that I should find a different job, anything at all, even a job as a prison guard. After the two months of summer vacation I tell myself again that being a secondary teacher at least trumps joining the five-million-strong ranks of the unemployed. The five-million-strong ranks of the unemployed is what sends me again on the bus and then the train for three hours a day to my three problem classes, my teenage pupils, who spend whole classes yawning and discussing steamy movies. They look at me, frustrated. Having snuck past the police for some cinematic steam a dozen times at least, these thirteen-year-old connoisseurs can tell there's some problem with me just at a glance. They gesture wildly with their arms and legs. They shriek with laughter. They toot. They hoot. They reprimand. I go to the library to find Freud. To see what Freud had to say. Was it already too late at twenty-seven. Is it already too late at thirty-nine. Freud tells me that twenty-seven is not too late, not too late even in Freud's time, a time when men and women at twenty-seven were already rotten with experience. But even Freud finds me beyond help. Stopped at twenty-eight. Restart at thirty-nine? It's impossible. Even Freud has never dreamed of it. Even Freud finds me beyond help. I don't dare go to the psychiatrists. They too would be wary of me. I'm incurable and they don't run a lab. The Ministry of Education who pays my wage couldn't pay them to study me, they know better than to get involved, I would hardly bring them any benefit, only the sure reputation of ineptitude. Even if I did go to them, I know they would try their best to receive me, lend me their ear for fifteen minutes, then have their secretary kindly show me the door. And if I darkened this door on another occasion, the secretary would helpfully book me an appointment slap-bang in the middle of Monday, impossible for me to travel thirty kilometers each way in time for my next class. If I should haunt them every Wednesday for every minute that they're open, insisting that I be examined, as stubborn as a mule, they would tell me to my face that there is no cure for my condition, which isn't even documented in the lists of the Ministry of Health, and which even Freud finds beyond help. At the door, by way of soothing me, the secretary will helpfully hand me a xeroxed list of associations twenty pages long. I am to spend a week poring over the list, to determine which one can help me best in my plight. The Asian immigrant association, or the single mom society, or the guild for teachers of the worst-performing secondary schools, or the alliance for victims of war, or the league of women approaching menopause, or maybe all five together. When I've taken my pick, I will then have to pay the joining fee, find a photo for my membership card, and send Vĩnh off to a neighbor's to go bare my heart at their weekly meetings, show up at their monthly parties, rent a bicycle and make sandwiches for their annual picnics, and if fellow members phone me every two or three days I shouldn't take it with bad grace, because the need for parties and picnics and heart-baring is always higher than expected. Then, in the spirit of psychology, I should find Vĩnh his own association. And pay his joining fee. And find a photo for his membership card. Unable to find one already existing, I would have to take him to a photo booth. Insert four one-euro coins, wait a few minutes, receive four 3 × 4 cm photos. And set aside one day a week, a different day than his Chinese class in rue Tolbiac, to take him to his association. And wait outside for two hours while he bares his heart to his fellow members. And take him to his monthly parties, paying for both his and my slots. And go with him to his yearly picnics, hiring two bicycles, packing two rounds of sandwiches. Now and then the phone would ring and there would be some unfamiliar boy or girl on the other end. The need for parties, picnics, and heart-baring is no less urgent among children than adults. I wonder where I can find the hours to waste on all those associations and meetings. My incurable condition will have to stay incurable, likely also staying outside the Ministry of Health's lists for decades to come. But then I tell myself, such an incurable, outside thing is not meant to be treated. We had so many outrageous diseases in Vietnam and the USSR, yet we still survived. If I can't write about sex, I will simply put it aside, I won't touch it, I'll write something else instead. Once a month I climb to the eighteenth floor in tour Olympiades to listen to the anecdotes of Mlle. Feng Xiao. Mlle. Feng Xiao has neither husband nor lover, but at fifty she still does nicely without a psychiatrist, the Asian immigrant association, or the league of women approaching menopause. She smiles if people tease her about her fifty-year-old maidenhood. She smiles if they threaten her with becoming a lonely, spiteful spirit in her afterlife. She smiles if they give her sincere advice that an old-age union with an old-age partner is still genuine old-age happiness. She makes no comment. She talks on about Sichuan her homeland, Sichuan of the celebrated white sardines that swim among lotus blossoms in the fish farm before lying among lotus blossoms at the feast, of the great connoisseur and overall great man Deng Xiao Ping, the greatest of all leaders of China. He passed away, poor fellow, in ailments and agony, poor fellow. Every time she mentions Deng Xiao Ping, she speaks in the same tone and says the same words. I guess that's her way to console herself. I feel for her. I tell her that Thụy is an Âu, my husband and Vĩnh's father is also an Âu. She smiles, so nĭ and I are related. The men of Âu clan are the most adventurous of China, the men of Âu clan travel all over the world. I tell her again that his hair is cropped and his eyes are slanted. She smiles again, the men of Âu clan are the handsomest of China, the men of Âu clan take wives all over the world. I smile back at her. I often think that he will have remarried. I don't write to him to ask. Neither do I ask his parents or Vĩnh. But I often imagine his new life with his new wife. I tell myself that I don't care about his private life. I tell myself that it's had nothing to do with me for a long long time. But still I often imagine how he is living with his new wife, how many children he has, whether he loves his new wife and new children. I cannot forget Chợ Lớn. I have never once been to Chợ Lớn. But still I can never forget Chợ Lớn. *The Lover* the movie left the haziest of impressions. *The North China Lover* is a jumble of mixed-up details in my memory. What I remember is the two-story house, the shop sign with Chinese lettering, the pair of lanterns. The photograph he sent on the day Vĩnh turned one. His photograph, which I often take out and gaze at. At Thụy, then at Vĩnh. To see when the two drops of water become indistinguishable. Vĩnh's birthday is next month. His father will call him when he turns twelve years old. I don't know why Thụy chooses that milestone. I don't know why he waits until now to dial my number, the number I have had for the last ten years, my only number since I moved to France. Vĩnh, who as a rule doesn't discuss his father with me, does not say anything, but I know he is counting the days. He has seen Thụy many times in Hà Nội. He has been familiar with his father's voice for the last three years. But he wants to hear him speaking from that faraway place, from a distance of many kilometers, Vĩnh doesn't know how many but he does know that it's far away, as far as the two-story house, the shop sign with Chinese lettering, the pair of lanterns. As seen in the photograph. His father's photograph, which he so often takes out and gazes at. At his father, then at himself. To see when the two drops of water become indistinguishable. He is counting the days. Never has his birthday been so significant. He asks me the time difference between Paris and Chợ Lớn. He does the math. He insists on taking the day off. He's afraid his father will call when he is at school. He demands that only he can pick up the phone that day. He wants to be the one who answers the call from his father. He wakes me up in the middle of the night and demands stories about Chợ Lớn. I tell him I know nothing of Chợ Lớn except the name. He says next Wednesday after Chinese class he will ask Hao Peng, Hao Peng has an answer for every question. He falls asleep. I lie sleepless beside him. I'm afraid. I'm afraid that at some point he will say he's had it up to here with Paris. He will say the same thing Thụy said to me. He will leave the same way Thụy left. He will pick the same day Thụy picked. The day he turned one month old. The day our marriage turned one year old. To leave. Those who want to leave always find an excuse. He will leave the same way Thụy left. The men of Âu clan are adventurous. The men of Âu clan travel the world. Mlle. Feng Xiao tells me, smiling. I lie on my bed, shivering. Vĩnh doesn't know that I'm afraid. Thụy didn't know that I was afraid, either. Not even I knew how afraid I was. Ever since my first night lying beside Thụy, for the first time, on our new bed. Or maybe it came earlier. On the riverbank, an hour after our wedding. Or even before that. Ever since I decided to marry him. Ever since I fell in love with him. I had known that he would leave. Quick as a flash. With no regret. At twenty-seven he had nothing to regret. At twenty-seven he still had personnel offices casting sideways glances at his Âu name. The personnel offices would seek the advice of their higher-ups in the Police Department. The Police Department would seek the advice of their higher-ups in the Home Office. The Home Office would seek the advice of their lower-downs in the counterespionage committee. The counterespionage committee would seek the advice of their lower-downs in the Chamber for Culture and Ideology. The Chamber for Culture and Ideology would seek the advice of their lower-downs in the agency for Chinese-ethnic surveillance. The agency for Chinese-ethnic surveillance would seek the advice of their lower-downs in the Hà Nội subagency. The Hà Nội subagency would seek the advice of their lower-downs in the Hoàn Kiếm district branch where we lived. Since his graduation from the University of Architecture, Thụy hadn't had a single opportunity to pick up his pencil. What he did make, during the twelve months of our life together, were one bookshelf, one cupboard, one table with a couple of little stools. Vĩnh turned one month old. For a whole week Thụy hadn't slept a wink. I hadn't slept a wink. We both waited. We both knew what we were waiting for. We both didn't dare say it out loud. We both didn't dare look at one another. If by any unfortunate chance we found ourselves face-to-face, our eyes automatically dropped to the ground. The same way I acted with my parents for the half year leading to our wedding. The difference is that in front of them, I never cried. In my parents' house it was taught that tears are useless. But with Thụy facing me across the dinner table, my eyes brimmed with tears as I held my bowl. What I put in my mouth was tear-soaked rice. Thụy couldn't bear it. He didn't dare look at me. The rice stuck in our throats. I didn't know if he cried. I didn't dare look at him. I'm afraid of other people's tears, especially if the other person is a man, and especially if it's Thụy. No sound could be heard in the eighteen-square-meter apartment. And no sound could be heard from Vĩnh. I gently shook him, but the baby lay very still. Not a month old yet, and he already knew how to keep silent. He too seemed to be waiting. For that something that Thụy and I both knew, but neither dared say out loud. Vĩnh had been waiting since the days he lived in my belly. They say that the fetus's heart beats to the rhythm of its mother's. The kitten Thụy bought on the day of our wedding had also left. The kitten couldn't bear the silence. The silence, and the tears. The silence made my body limpid. The tears twisted my face. A week before Thụy got on the Thống Nhất. Our mirror turned its back to us. It kept its back turned I don't know how long. Until the day I sat for the postgraduate exams. Until the day I boarded the plane. Even now, in my Belleville apartment, the mirror frequently turns its back to us. I don't need it to tell me I have been wearing a twisted face for the last twelve years. An impassive face, as my pupils often reprimand me. A sullen face, as the guy often remarks. A stress-inducing face, as my colleagues often say behind my back. I don't want the whole school to explode in a collective fit of stress, so when they have their break I stay in the classroom, when they have lunch in the cafeteria I sit in the staff room chewing my sandwich. I never go to the cafeteria to announce that this blouse or these shoes I'm wearing were bought in Auchan in last July's sales, to debate the merits of gas heaters vs. oil or electric, to ask which IT-savvy colleague can help unfreeze my home computer, presumably a victim of the peculiar virus that has infected twenty thousand Parisian computers, as was announced on television yesterday. And I never pay five euros a term for the right to put my own mug in the staff room, so that whenever I'm thirsty I can add a spoonful of coffee and two sugar blocks, pour on some boiled water and drink, all the while complaining that someone has used my mug by mistake and demanding the culprit be brought to justice, then put up on the wall a sheet of paper with neatly printed big letters: one should only drink from one's own mug. The next day a new line is guaranteed to appear on the sheet, no less big and no less neat: what an interesting suggestion. The next day again an illustration is sure to come, a mug and a mouth complete with teeth and tongue, connected by an equals sign, very square, very red. At the end of each month they take down forty-nine such suggestions by the school's forty-nine teachers, forty-nine very interesting suggestions in neatly printed big letters, always illustrated and always heartily supported. I don't have anything to suggest. "Noël 2004, Noël du Vietnam" would be silly. It's likely that the next day someone would add to it: "50 years of Điện Biên Phủ, 50 nem." And the next day again someone else would draw an illustration, a cannon and a roll of nem, of the same size and emitting the same thick plumes of smoke, connected by an equals sign, very square, very red. I don't have anything to suggest. I don't have their habit of making suggestions. I'm afraid that my Southeast Asian suggestions would be too Southeast Asian-y. Not in ten years have I been able to come up with any suggestion Western European enough to garner my colleagues' hearty support. In these ten years I have passed through who knows how many Parisian suburbs. The train cars with me their sole occupant, dozing. The platforms vanishing into mist. The ticket booths with windows not yet drawn up. The mileposts all misshapen. The meadows of grass upon dense grass. So black and stretching on forever. Beyond the horizon there may lie my country. My country shaped like an S. Huế as its middle point. Hà Nội above. Sài Gòn beneath. And next to Sài Gòn, Chợ Lớn. Or Cholen in the writings of Duras. Or Chinatown as the Americans call it, and the French who follow suit, happy with how it sounds. Beyond the horizon. Right or left. East or west. I can't tell for sure. My sense of direction leaves much to be desired. Three times I took the driving test and three times I failed. I don't know if it's a good idea to take it a fourth time. Or to borrow money from the bank and buy a car in installments. I don't even know where I'd put one if I did. There's no basement parking where I live. Don't even think about it if you live in Belleville. Every week several notes appear in my mailbox asking me to give up my parking spot, their unknown sender unknowing that I have nothing to give up. Even if I do buy a car, what can I use it for. Forget about driving to work; I can't sprout wings to fly to school at will, and even one traffic jam on the motorway would lead to my colleagues again erupting in a collective fit of stress, my teenage pupils blocking my doorway at the beginning of the next class and reprimanding me. I could drive on holidays, but again I don't know where to go, whom to visit; every part of France is equally beautiful, equally alien to me, places I have only ever seen on postcards. I've worked ten years in the education system and still I'm not used to the various holidays. I can't tell the Normandy sea from the Mediterranean, can't remember which one is shark-infested and which isn't, which is bitter and which is salty. I don't know what season is best for mushroom hunting, which kinds are edible and which are poisonous. And I can't see why people want to huff and puff their way up to some summit just to come skiing down again, just for the chance to break their arms, dislocate their knees, burst their arteries, suffer their heart attacks. Life in France remains abstract, just the same as when I first arrived. At the Immigration Office, they shake their heads when I tell them in all honesty that I want to be naturalized so I won't have to stand in line from eight to five to pay fifty euros to get to stay another eleven months and twenty-nine days. They shake their heads again when I reply that no, Vĩnh and I don't speak French at home, don't know which is the fork hand and which the knife, don't decorate a tree when the Gregorian year comes to an end nor go to the Maison de la Mutualité's Tết gala with our fellow Vietnamese. They shake and shake their heads. They show me the door and shake my hand: hang in there do your best. Every year I request a day off to take the Métro to the Cité, get into the enormous elevator at the station and then submerge myself in the throng of people streaming toward the Police Prefecture. After ten years, I know most of the resident permit renewal office's staff by sight. One of the women is very young, with long legs and beringed hands. The last time I saw her, a wedding ring had been added to the collection. Another has a square jaw and short hair, and never smiles. Seems to be in charge. Seems never to see any visitors. Another, of mysterious age, has a perm and is always in a white short-sleeved T-shirt. It was she who saw me the first time I came, my first year in France. Your documents, all of them, she said, her voice listless, her upper eyelids about to drop at any moment. I was afraid. I felt my stomach turn. Even back in Hà Nội, I always felt my stomach turn whenever I found myself in the hospital or the police station. My command of French at the time was miserable, so my stomach turned really hard. She suddenly went out and I was left alone. I was bewildered. I didn't know if I'd said something to offend her. Or if there was something wrong with my papers. Or if she had gone to the next room to seek the advice of her higher-ups, and her higher-ups had sought the advice of the Foreign Office at

Quai d'Orsay, and the Foreign Office had sought the advice of the Home Office of the country concerned, and the phone had rung thirty times unanswered. I considered running out to find her and let her know that four p.m. in Paris means ten p.m. in Vietnam, the old guard would be either watching a football game or sawing some logs until the Home Office staff woke him up a half day later. I wondered if I should wait for another half day or leave for the kindergarten to pick up Vĩnh, whose sore throat had endured for a few days. I'd spent two hours squirming on the hard chair when the lady in the white T-shirt came back. Her eyelids still about to drop at any moment. She took up my papers and resumed reading as if nothing whatsoever had happened. My stomach resumed its turning. I wanted to excuse myself to run to the bathroom. But my command of French was miserable. I didn't dare speak up. I was afraid that I would offend her. I didn't dare look at her face, her white T-shirt, or her white fingers. My face was as miserable as my French, and equally likely to offend. My stomach turned. My stomach turned some serious somersaults. My stomach turned for another half hour when again she got up and left for who knows where. I had still not recovered when she came back and held out my passport. Her upper eyelids still about to drop at any moment. I panicked. I imagined that the old guard in the Home Office of my country, during a ten-minute break in the match between the Police of Sài Gòn and the Port of Hải Phòng, had reached out for his thuốc lào pipe, and while lighting the tobacco abruptly become aware of the phone then ringing its thirtieth ring. Thanks to the French lessons in his three years at Nam Định secondary school, he knew enough to say oui and non to Mrs. Secretary at Quai d'Orsay. Then she had somehow utilized her thirty-years' worth of secretarial experience to send him flying to the archive room, where my files were found in under a minute, on top of ten other sets of files on Hà Nội's ten ethnically Chinese families who had faith in the party. Mrs. Secretary at Quai d'Orsay would then have thanked the Home Office of the home country for their amicable cooperation, hoped to see the guard another time, and called her higher-ups to give a report. I imagined newly stamped words in my passport, in fresh red ink: residence permit rejected for internal reasons. Tomorrow Vĩnh and I would go to the airport, putting an end to our three-month-and-two-day stay in France. My parents would weep copiously when I told them the news over the phone tonight. Their two soaked handkerchiefs would remain unwrung. This time they would be ill for real. So ill they wouldn't go to Nội Bài to pick up me and Vĩnh, the returnees from paradise, so ill they wouldn't be able to do anything, even get up and go to the end of the street to buy fifty grams of lean pork for Vĩnh's sore-throat porridge. Someone pulled at the chair I was sitting on. Someone told me to move so that other people could get their business done. Someone threw the stack of papers at me that I'd let fall on the floor. I managed to forget Vĩnh's sore throat for a moment to say goodbye to that someone and to the lady in the white T-shirt. I didn't know if they returned my goodbye. I was breathlessly admiring my first ever French temporary residence card. My name, Vĩnh's name, our family name—Thụy's family name, and our dates of birth, and our address in Belleville, and the day we'd arrived at Charles de Gaulle, everything a hundred percent correct. I didn't walk but flew out of the Police Prefecture. I paused to play with the parrot in front of the pet bird shop by the Métro gates. I was delighted to hear it say nı˅ ha˙o. Must have been some recent tourists from Taiwan. I got into the enormous elevator, my stomach now completely tranquil. Once home I admired my residence card some more, and wished I'd taught the parrot to say xin chào. If it didn't bungle it and call me a Shih Tzu I would then teach it to say zdravstvuite. The next year, I was seen again by the white T-shirt lady. She hadn't changed a bit. Still with the perm. Still with the upper eyelids about to drop at any moment. Your documents, all of them, she said, in the same listless voice as before. I was afraid. My stomach began to turn. My stomach turned some serious somersaults when she got up and left for who knows where. Later I learned she had a habit of going to the next room for a cup of coffee, probably to ward off drowsiness. If the coffee didn't perk her up, she would try a phone call instead. With her listless voice. And her upper eyelids about to drop at any moment. Probably she would call her friend a few offices over, who had also just drunk a perk-me-up. And probably both ladies would then take a nap, meaning every day a few more foreigners would contemplate calling an ambulance for their serious bout of somersaulting stomach. The loveliest clerk on the Île de la Cité in my opinion is a plump, tender-voiced older lady of color. My papers once had the good fortune to fall into her hands. I'd forgotten my certificate of employment signed by the headmaster. I said I would go home to get it. I didn't live too far away. I lived in Belleville. The lady simply waved a dismissive hand. She proceeded to give me an extension. Last year, by chance, I saw her on the Métro. I wanted to go up to her and say hi, how do you do, then give her a smile and leave, no disruption, no bribery. But I hesitated. And held back. She must see many Asian women every day, a great deal of whom must have forgotten their certificates of employment, tenancy agreements, wage slips for the last three months, annual income tax receipts, latest electricity bills, water bills, phone bills. The Police Prefecture announces their list of required documents well beforehand, but Asian women always give an apologetic smile for forgetting something, always call a taxi home to look for something, always take out their mobile phones to ask a family member to please come on your motorbike here and bring me those papers. I hesitated. I didn't say hi. And she didn't recognize me. We just passed each other by. I'd forgotten about my citizenship application. I hadn't heard from the Immigration Office since my last interview. I was content to be a Vietnamese citizen, to request a day off every year to go to the Île de la Cité. I don't imagine that I'll be back some day just because of the parrot who says nǐ hǎo. Tomorrow I turn thirty-nine. The same age as the protagonist of *I'm Yellow*. He has just finalized his divorce and is now hanging around at Hàng Cỏ station. At first I wanted them to be a woman. Then I had second thoughts. I was afraid that Phượng of *Made in Vietnam* would come back and badger me about it. For a few months now she has been knocking at my door. Won't you let me be your protagonist again, she would say. That stubborn thing somehow won, sneaking into two of my short stories. Not that I wasn't aware. But this time I must be firm. To sever all ties to Phượng, I will join him on the train from Hà Nội. But I haven't decided yet where we will go. Sài Gòn won't do; Phượng has alighted both at Bình Triệu station and Tân Sơn Nhất airport. Huế, I ruled out right from the start. I found its violetness disturbing. Next to be ruled out was Đà Lạt. Another unbearably violet city. For several lunch breaks now I have been reading Vietnamese online newspapers. My country is changing day by day. Even the northeast and northwest are now unbearably violet. As unbearably violet as their orchid trees. The orchid tree is now ubiquitous in our short stories, long stories, socioromantic movies, contemporary fine art, chamber music, and who knows what else. Of all the big and small towns from north to south, I don't know which we should choose to get off at. After twenty-nine years of unification they've all become siblings under the same roof, so that three hundred townships have launched three hundred shrimp export initiatives, burnt three hundred chicken factories with gasoline in the bird flu epidemic, organized three hundred night galas to celebrate fifty years since the victory in Điện Biên, all called "By the water of the Nậm Rốm we sing." All the towns between the stations of Hàng Cỏ and Bình Triệu—

Ninh Bình, Thanh Hóa or Vinh, Đồng Hới, Tam Kỳ, Quảng Ngãi, Quy Nhơn, Phan Thiết...—are his to choose from, and I let him have full control over all his decisions. I don't believe in imprisoning my characters inside wooden frames to put under glass and hang on my wall. He will see that I'm willing and able to jump off at any of the thirty stations the Thống Nhất calls at. If he then wants to take a bus all the way to Buôn Mê Thuột, and from there all the way up to Đắc Lắc, I will never complain of carsickness. I will go behind him for the whole month or the whole year. Airplane or bus, bike taxi or train or ship, I will never ask for a barf bag or a sickness pill. He will find me a most faithful companion. Seventeen years of sweet catjang soup and pot-steamed pig brains in Hà Nội. Five years of cabbage with mutton in the Leningrad State University cafeteria. Another ten years of instant noodles for breakfast, sandwiches for lunch, and a choice of the two for dinner, in Paris and the surrounding areas. My cuisine CV is unrivaled. As for comfort, he need only be concerned for himself. My extensive training has left me able to nod off for the three commuting hours every day, whether in the drowsiest lulls or in the middle of the most dramatic transportation changes. And I'm no stranger to power loss in the middle of a meal, hot water loss in the middle of a shower, heaters giving up the ghost in the middle of a subzero night. He will find that I have no talents to speak of, only the talent of being the easiest companion ever. He will also find that I'm open to anything, anything but turning him into Thụy, anything but following him to Chợ Lớn. I don't want to write about Thụy. I spend a lot of effort not to write about him. Writing to me is not an act of reminiscence. Nor is it an act of oblivion. Not until my last novel will I know why I write. Not until my last novel will I be able to understand him. My last novel will be dedicated to him. Thụy is a mystery. I have loved him as a mystery, the mystery to end all mysteries. Yên Khê will forever remain the primal mystery. Yên Khê. He wasn't born in Hà Nội, in the national ob-gyn hospital like me, or, like most of the children on my street, the maternity clinic by the banyan tree of the old cow house. Yên Khê. You'll have to study hard to make up for that trip. My parents gave in to an unexpected indulgence. Yên Khê. We let student Âu Phương Thụy go on the school camping trip, though it's our duty to ensure that he's watched closely. The ideology teacher unexpectedly let his guard down. Yên Khê. So that his sleeping head could come to rest on my shoulder. So that no five Russian years could erase from memory. So that even now an unquietness. Yên Khê. Never have I heard a name more strange. Thụy took me back to Yên Khê. Yên Khê. Yên Khê. On the bus I asked him why. He smiled, even his Chinese could not tell him why. Why. I was silent. I thought Yên Khê was fate. Every fate is a mystery. I thought about fate at twenty-seven. Was it early or was it late. Boys and girls playing tug-of-war. So fervently did they pull. The cord snapped. They all clapped like thunder. But Thụy and I, at the head of our respective lines, fell forward and crashed into each other. My glasses smashed to pieces. His face was speckled with blood. My mother stamped her feet, camping is the most useless thing in the world. My father ground his teeth, you will never again participate in any such uselessness. Yên Khê was my last useless thing. Yên Khê was also my first sleepless night. Was it chance or was it fate. Yên Khê. We sat on a bank, the river not wide enough, the water not clear enough, he not brave enough to talk to me, I not brave enough to touch his fingers, the most exquisite fingers I had ever seen, and our nights out from then on were always the same, on the bank of the Red River which was never wide enough, its waters never clear enough, sitting side by side in silence. Yên Khê. After all the tents had been packed up, the school body gathered under a banyan tree. The radio was put in the middle. The announcer lady, choking up: Chinese gunners just now fired five cannonballs into the town of Đồng Đăng. The literature teacher, choking up: home of the bustling Kỳ Lừa market, of the faithful lady Tô Thị, of the cave pagoda of Tam Thanh. The history teacher, choking up: morning stream and nighttime cave, President Hồ's Pác Pó cave is right next door to Đồng Đăng. The geography teacher, choking up: the road to Hà Nội is one hundred and fifty kilometers from Đồng Đăng, but as the bird flies it's only one hundred. The whole school, choking up: Yên Khê is one and a half hours by car from Hà Nội. The whole school, choking up, looked at Thụy. I turned to look at the ground. I was afraid that he would burst into tears. And that I would follow suit. I would cry so hard, now that my eyes were naked without my glasses. He too would cry so hard, the bandage on his face would melt in his tears. Between us we would force the whole school to put their hands over their ears. There would no more be choking up on the radio. It would spontaneously switch itself to another channel. The announcer, all smiles and sunshine, would welcome us to her on-demand music hour. The first song to be heard would be Việt Nam Chi Na mountain to mountain river to river. Performed by singer Trung Kiên, at the request of teachers and students from the town of Đồng Đăng. The teachers and students from the town of Đồng Đăng would like to dedicate this song to cannon gunners in both Vietnam and China. The whole school would clap the rhythm. The ideology teacher would clap the hardest. His nickname was Mr. Claps. He would keep clapping even when everyone else had stopped. He claims that ideology is expressed through enthusiastic clapping. From Yên Khê the bus went back to Hà Nội, bus and riders both rocking to the rhythm of Việt Nam Chi Na. The radio itself rocked. Potholes in the road made the rocking even more vigorous. The driver rocked as if possessed by a spirit, the literature teacher and the history teacher and the geography teacher as if possessed as well. People's Artist

Trung Kiên sang at the service of his people for an hour and a half without letup. Ten years later the ideology teacher still looked back fondly upon the day, at every school anniversary he would tell how that camping trip to Yên Khê had witnessed unprecedented clapping from both teachers and students, unprecedented ideological zeal. Ten years later, I said that at the time I'd wished I was Chinese-Vietnamese so that the whole school could choke up and stare at both of us as they pleased. Thụy said that at the time he'd wanted to turn into an ant and run to hide in the banyan tree. I joked that he was a Chinese-Vietnamese ant. He smiled. I joked again that I would follow wherever he went, I would be a girl ant climbing the banyan tree after him. He smiled again. I joked that I would carry my baby ant on my back and trudge after him for the rest of my life. He just kept on smiling. I love to look at his smile. His smile is as strange as anything about him. He took me here and there around the campsite, but he avoided the banyan tree. That withered old man of a banyan tree. Lightning had cut off its head. I didn't dare go near it either. Surely it was home to at least a few ghosts, fighting among themselves for a dwelling. There was surely a female ghost grinding its teeth night after night, unable to thwart the four eighteen-year-olds who either were martyred in the resistance war against the French, or perished in the one against the Americans, or expired in a recent Chinese-bike race around the town lake. I lived in Russia for five years. In Russian winters the trees themselves turned into snow. But I had never seen anything like the banyan trees of my homeland. I have lived in France for ten years. My pupils didn't lack for extraordinary fates. But I have never seen any fate like Thụy's. Life is hard for a Vietnamese, and life is hard for a Chinese, but none is hard in quite the way it is for a Chinese-Vietnamese. Mlle. Feng Xiao said that in 1980 the province of Sichuan took in eighty Chinese-Vietnamese families. The eighty families were distributed among eighty cooperatives. Mlle. Feng Xiao's received one.

Meek as mice. Poor things. The wife and the three children didn't know a single word of Chinese. They just sat and wept all day. Everyone who saw them felt pity for them. Everyone who saw them told them, Yuenan folk just need to take the train to Kunming, from Kunming the train to Guangdong, from Guangdong the ferry to Nanning, from Nanning hop on a long-distance truck and you'll be back in Yuenan. No one knew if the family understood a word they were told. They only sat and wept all day. Pitiful things. As pitiful as my dream the other night. Thụy took baby Vĩnh back to Hunan on his bicycle. I cycled after him, carrying a twenty-liter can of lard. Mlle. Feng Xiao said that in 1980 a liter of lard was worth half the monthly wage of a public servant in Sichuan. The village police said they didn't know who Thụy was. He declared his father's and grandfather's names. They looked these up in the civil registry. They shook their heads, grandfather and father both passed away over thirty years ago. Thụy demanded to be taken to the old Âu family house. At the gate twenty families ran out. A chorus of twenty families rose up. The house is full of beds, the garden is full of beds, there's half the dumpsite left, you can put your bed there, there are a few hoes left, you can each take one to hoe with, when you're done remember to put them back, when you're done with that remember to give a liter of lard to each family. Vĩnh's first strike of the hoe went straight into his foot. Thụy ran to the hospital with the boy on his back. I ran after them, trying to memorize the way so I could come back later, put on a rice pot, and get the boy's toothbrush. He cried so hard. I cried so hard. The nurse ran out, took one look at us and ran back inside. Half an hour later, still no one had come with needle and thread to sew Vĩnh's foot. He cried harder. I cried harder. Thụy ran into the hospital and demanded to see the director of the children's limb-sewing department. The old guard shook his head, Yuenan children's limb, go back to Yuenan to sew. Thụy said he was not Yuenanese, the child was not Yuenanese either. The guard looked at me and shook his head again. Crying, I said I was not Yuenanese either. He still shook his head. Crying, I shouted, bù shì yuènán rén. He shook his head even more. Crying, I explained that I too was an Âu. You don't believe it, you can see my residence card. Thụy got on the train to Sài Gòn at night and the very next morning the whole neighborhood was alive with the news of us coming to blows, the court giving me the apartment to raise Vĩnh. But at the French embassy I have been madame Âu from the moment I showed up in the visa office. In Belleville I have been madame Âu for the last ten years, comment ça va madame Âu. The doorman says here's some China letter for you madame Âu. The doorman, who is from Portugal, thinks Hà Nội is a suburb of Beijing. On the Île de la Cité the loudspeaker asks madame Âu to please come to window no. 14. The lady in the white T-shirt asks for madame Âu's documents, all of them. In the secondary schools I work at, the vice-headmasters and headmasters running into me would shake my hands in a friendly manner, do your best madame Âu. My forty-nine colleagues and my teenage pupils call me madame Âu to my face, while behind my back they say la chinoise, la chinoise bizarre. You only need to say la chinoise and the whole school would know who you're talking about. Bù shì yuènán rén. I'm not Vietnamese. I explained. I cried. I shouted so loud Vĩnh woke up and asked, what awful language is mom speaking. For a whole month I dreamed that Thụy took me and Vĩnh back to Hunan. Every dream was just as pitiful as the first. Later the twenty-liter can of lard was replaced by a pair of scarlet wedding sedge mats. Mlle. Feng Xiao says Hunan is on the border with Mongolia, where sedge can't grow. In Hunan people sleep on jute rugs. I was afraid that Vĩnh would hurt his back. The pair of mats were tied to my bicycle rack, one for him to sleep on now, the other to put away for the future. Who knows when I would have another chance to go to Hàng Chiếu the Sedge Mat Street to buy him a new pair. Once I dreamed all three of us were sitting on the scarlet mat having dinner, the can of lard beside us, but Vĩnh and I just held our chopsticks, not eating. Vĩnh was crying and asking for roast pigeon. I said to Thụy, there's a tiny patch of land next to the dumpsite, how about we plant some vine spinach and jute seeds. Thụy nodded, a daily diet of boiled dumplings stuffed with nothing but preserved cabbage can blister any tongue. His tongue was not Yuenanese, but it still longed for vine spinach and jute soup plus two pickled Vietnamese eggplants. I pouted, vine spinach and jute shoot down your throat straight to your stomach, even Vĩnh's swollen throat can handle it. Thụy and I each took a hoe to work the soil. Vĩnh, his foot still in stitches, lay reading *Journey to the West*, the episode where Sun Wu Kong fights Lady White Bone. After hoeing, I mixed the fine-cut food scraps in and covered the mix in a careful, very biologically correct fashion. A week later Thụy went out to sow, a seed for each hole, twenty holes a row, five rows in total. All three of us spent our mornings weeding, afternoons watering, and evenings watching the weather report. If rain was due the next day, the night before we would build four levees around the patch so that the hundred seeds wouldn't swim to the dumpsite. When new skin began to grow on Vĩnh's foot, he was given a stick to chase birds away. A week later, the hundred seeds had grown into a hundred seedlings. After another week, the hundred seedlings had shed their seed leaves and grown new leaves. Thụy and I were busy weeding, three rows for him and two for me. When the weeding was done, we equipped ourselves with a bucket and a dipper each. By the time the sun set, the hundred seedlings would each have received a dipperful of rainwater mixed with Vĩnh's pee. His foot was now fully healed. Once he chased away a mob of eagles who were after the seedlings. Jubilant, Thụy and I could think about nothing else but the bowl of vine spinach and jute soup. Every day I promised Vĩnh this was the last time we would have boiled cabbage dumplings for dinner. One morning, the three of us were jolted awake by the racket outside. Vĩnh grabbed his stick and ran out. Our garden had disappeared under that mob of eagles, and what last night had been a hundred seedlings had turned into a hundred cabbage heads, identical to the hundred plastic-wrapped cabbage heads piled in a pyramid in the Leningrad food store. Vĩnh wailed. His sore throat had been acting up for the last few days, he was so looking forward to the vine spinach and jute soup that would shoot down his throat into his stomach. Half a year later we still hadn't finished preserving the cabbages, which we needed to give to our twenty neighbors in exchange for twenty meals of boiled dumplings. I told my dream about the vine spinach and jute soup to Mlle. Feng Xiao on the first Sunday of the following month. She had a great laugh over it. She said, Hunan is on the border with Mongolia, even cabbages cannot grow, let alone those Yuenan veggie of nı̆. She laughed and laughed. When she finally stopped, she promised next time she would give me a charm to fend off dreams. You have all those dreams in your head, you won't be able to sleep. I wonder if I really should put her charm up at the head of my bed. The picture with the two-story house, the shop sign with Chinese lettering, the pair of lanterns, has delivered me from my obsession with Thụy's death. I no longer see him jumping from a train, hanging himself, or eating poisonous mushrooms in my dreams. For the last twelve years our family of three has been together in every one of my dreams, whether accompanied by a moment of sadness or a full night of joviality. I wonder whether those dreams are really as bad for me as Mlle. Feng Xiao seems to think. I wonder too whether they haven't long become an integral part of my life. Whether my left eye won't twitch nonstop if they go missing even for a night. If they go missing even for a night, I would surely end up misplacing my glasses or forgetting my keys. I love most the dreams that last from the night right until seven a.m., when the first passengers get on the train and I hurriedly take out a textbook, which I read less than I rub my eyes, because a few more minutes of dreaming probably means missing the stop for the connecting bus. I love too the dreams that blend night into day and day into night, over the two months of summer holiday, when Vĩnh is back in Vietnam and there's not a soul on the whole floor, not a ghost of a light in the whole block, even the doorman has gone back to Portugal, and only once every few days something slips into my mailbox, and never anything asking me to give up my parking spot. And then there are short dreams that come suddenly when I am sitting alone in the staff room, half a sandwich still in my hand. Thụy and Vĩnh would be watching a football match, and I would be in charge of the remote control, cheering on the Chamber of Commerce team from Mlle. Feng Xiao's Sichuan and keeping an eye out in case my forty-nine colleagues tiptoe in from the door. There was one where all three of us were asleep, Vĩnh in the middle, his left leg resting on my belly, his right weighing down his father's thigh. The phone rang, I scrambled to pick it up. After my third "hello," Yamina and Yasin's mother burst into tears on the other end. Not knowing what to do, I burst into tears myself. Vĩnh grumbled, what awful news is mom getting. Thụy woke up too. He ran into the bathroom, soaked a towel under the tap and brought it to me. I wiped my eyes and pouted, okay let's all go back to sleep. Vĩnh was snoring after a minute, but Thụy and I tossed and turned before each getting up for a sleeping pill. The next day, I went into the staff room, put my briefcase down, lined my stomach with a bite of sandwich and promptly unplugged the telephone. Twenty-four hours later, a sheet of paper appeared on the wall, on which someone had neatly printed the words: respect common property as your own. Another twenty-four hours again, another colleague had added: an instruction full of goodwill. Yet another twenty-four hours, a third colleague had provided an illustration of the staff room's boxy phone and the Nokia mobile I'd bought last month, connected by an equals sign, very square, very red. The shortest dream, lasting under a minute, came right in the middle of class. Thụy and I took Vĩnh to Thủ Lệ zoo, but the boy had barely taken a bite of his green rice ice cream when he was snatched away by an eighteen-month-old gorilla. I covered my face with my hands and cried in fear. My pupils, stunned, turned to look at me. They forgot their discussion on steamy movies, which had just reached its climax. They each took a notebook and pen from their bags. They looked at me in silence. I cried harder. They looked at each other, perplexed. They didn't dare look at me. Laboriously they copied down the date. I wiped my tears and said, class is over, there's no homework. They put their notebooks and pens back into their bags. Yamina raised her hand and asked if there would be an oral test the next day. I was busy watching Vĩnh, who was executing some kung fu move to wrestle with the gorilla. I didn't know how to answer her. The pupils sprang up. They protested. I had no right to give a test when I hadn't completed the lesson, whether oral or written it's against pedagogical laws, they argued. I was worrying that Thụy hadn't told the zookeepers to put real bullets in their guns, the gorilla would strangle Vĩnh. I covered my face and cried. They were stunned. They looked at one another, perplexed. They forgot to threaten to report me to the vice-headmaster and headmaster. I was still afraid. My glasses were wet with tears. They stood up, took their bags and hats, and left. Yamina stayed behind. She took out her handkerchief to wipe my glasses, and when she was done she asked me if it was a very bad dream. I was silent. She said her mom often had such dreams. Her mom dreamed that her father took the whole family on a trip to the Sahara. Her mom found a cactus and was about to wring it for some water to cook rice when the camel Yasin was riding slipped. Her mom looked back just in time to see its four legs disappear into a forty-meter-deep sandpit. She covered her face and cried. Cried and urged Yasin to jump. Cried and thrashed on the bed. She often wakes her two children up at night to tell them about her wedding to their father, how he rode in on a two-humped camel, wearing a silk vest, with an English cigarette hanging from his lips, and put a string of jade beads around her neck. At the end of each year, Yamina's mom tells Yasin to call his father and ask after him, how he is living with his new wife, how many children he has, whether he loves his new wife and new children. Yamina and I hugged each other in the classroom and cried. I too often imagine how Thụy is living with his new wife, how many children he has, whether he loves his new wife and new children. I couldn't stop crying. Again Yamina took out her handkerchief to wipe my glasses. The vice-headmaster winked at me as he passed by my classroom: what a nice pupil, eh. The next morning, the staff room displayed a one-meter-square piece of cardboard, on which someone had neatly printed the words, as big as an official slogan: teachers should be mirrors in which children see their best selves. I looked down to my xeroxing job, and then looked up to see a new line added underneath, no less big and no less neat: most heartfelt advice of the year. I waved a dismissive hand. At lunchtime, when I walked in, even before putting down my briefcase, even before taking a bite of my sandwich to relieve my hunger then having a shortish dream to relieve my sleepiness, I saw my own face, moon-round, looming on the cardboard, tears streaming down it, and next to it the aspiring artist had added a mirror, equally moon-round, surrounded by a halo of spiky rays, the two circles of identical size connected by an equals sign, very square, very red. The meter-squared cardboard stayed on the wall. At the end of the month, they deemed it too precious to be taken down. They said it was the result of a collaboration among the school's forty-nine teachers, it was even better than an art project, it deserved to sit on the wall until the end of the year. Four p.m. on a Sunday. The guy called me on the phone. You have such a sullen face. Turns out it's only sullen toward me. Turns out you cry in front of your pupils every week. The parents' association is protesting against you on the Internet, clearly stating your name, your school, the classes you teach. Your tears make weaklings out of their children, they argue. They threaten to report you to the vice-director and director of the Ministry of Education. I waved a dismissive hand, I can always quit my job. There's an ad that runs on television every day, the Home Office is looking for prison guards, unbeatable benefits. When the ruling from the Ministry of Education arrives, I will quit my job then and there. I will return the six sets of test answers to the library, the six cassette tapes to the administrative staff, and the six keys to the school gates, still in their original six plastic bags, to the guard room. I will put them in six separate packets, place these in six Styrofoam boxes, address them, affix six special-class stamps, then take the lot to Belleville post office to throw into six postboxes. I will never again have to wait in line for my monthly train ticket, traipse to school at six a.m., plod to the staff room at high noon, chew a sandwich while looking out for a new heartfelt suggestion full of goodwill, especially for my tears. Once my twenty-four hours a day and thirty days a month are mine to deal with as I see fit, I will draw up a schedule as solid as if cast in concrete, so distinguished that even if I fax it to my parents they can only fax back a word of admiration. Every day we will get up at six a.m., I and Vīnh. After the morning routine, we will have a six-course breakfast: cake, butter, omelet, ham, sausage, orange juice. The six dishes anglaises will be concluded with tea mixed with six types of jam. Another sixty minutes later, Vīnh will have gone to school, and I will have ridden the bus to rue Tolbiac to practice my six-days-a-week Qigong and Taijiquan. When the martial arts classes finish at noon, I will stay behind to take a bath with six fragrance oils, then drink six kinds of sugarcane honey with my six shifus and sixty fellow disciples. Six minutes later I will be at Mlle. Feng Xiao's hair salon. I will teach her six words of Yuenanese. She will teach me six new words of Mandarin in return. From tour Olympiades I will push the elevator button, and six minutes later I'll be standing on the marble floor of the supermarket Tang Frères. The sixty buildings of Chinatown will be busy wrapping nem, spreading bánh cuốn, and kneading har gow, so I will take six pigeons produced by Ho Chi Minh City Food ImEx from the frozen aisle and bring them to the counter in less than six minutes. After sixty minutes on the bus from the gate of Tang Frères to Belleville, the six frozen pigeons will have thawed out nicely. Back at home I will immediately turn the oven to two hundred and sixty degrees. At six p.m. Vĩnh will come home from school, wash, and sit down to share with me the six roast pigeons marinated in húng lìu and six spoons of fried rice. He will drink sixty milliliters of Coca-Cola while I down sixty milliliters of red wine. After dinner and a dessert of six kinds of fruit and six-vitamin yogurt, we will turn on the television and switch to channel M6 for updates on the war in Iraq. Sixty minutes later, when Vĩnh has done reading the latest news online from the People's Republic of China, I will sit down at my computer. After writing sixty sentences and six words, I will turn off the light, take off my socks and climb into my bed. Minus my tossing and turning, my sixty-minute dream in the middle of the night and another six-minute dream at dawn, I will be guaranteed a full six hours of sleep. I will call it A Schedule of Six and Sixty. I will practice it religiously for six months. Then I will send my CV to the Home Office. Six days later, they will invite me for an interview. With my sixty kilograms in weight and six-year experience in education, not to mention my six foreign languages including the ultrarare Chinese and Vietnamese, and my six Qigong and Taijiquan belts, I will easily prevail over my sixty opponents. They will take me to choose a six-room apartment so that Vĩnh will have one room for his Internet, one for his table tennis, one for his kung fu. They will ask me if my preference among six types of car is Renault or Peugeot. They will tell me six times to write an application declaring what suits me best regarding my monthly salary, my annual leave, my age of retirement. It will all be as smooth as six uncles bedding six aunts. I waved a dismissive hand. I told the guy I was not afraid. He could be stressed for my sake all he liked. I was fully prepared. The Schedule of Six and Sixty took care of every single sixty-second block. From the Ministry of Education I will make six glorious jumps to the Home Office. Sixteen years later I will make a graceful exit, with a golden pension book in my hand. Vĩnh will be in the Gulf as a branch representative. If he can find me a job as interpreter, all the better, my six characters can expand their network. Or if Vietnamese businessmen have not yet parachuted into Baghdad, or if they have but have elected to approach partners on their own and draw up contracts in our mother tongues, I will stay at home taking care of Vĩnh, my golden pension book won't be any less golden, and my six characters will climb onto camels, maps in their hands and packs on their backs, making sixty rounds of the Sahara. Every day I will bring home six pigeons to marinate in húng lìu and roast and share with Vĩnh. I will plant sixty square meters of vine spinach and jute. The climate in the Gulf is similar enough to Hà Nội's. No need to weed or chase away birds, no need of rainwater mixed with pee, the plants will all grow to be sixty centimeters high. After six years as a brand representative, Vĩnh will have forgotten what a sore throat feels like. I had everything prepared. I had plans for every outcome. I waited and waited and waited, but no minister of education wrote to me. Yamina had found six chances to say goodbye to me, giving me six handkerchiefs so that in my new place I would have something to wipe my glasses with. Her mom had called me in the staff room six times, still sobbing without being able to say anything, still somehow always right at six a.m. when all three of us were asleep, Vĩnh in the middle, his left leg resting on my belly, his right weighing down his father's thigh. Six days later Yasin brought me a bag of food prepared by his mom so that I could quickly gain the last sixteen kilograms needed. I opened it to find six birds spreading their wings on emerald-green leaves, some unknown vegetable. Later I found in a library six books on North African cuisine. The pigeon seasoned with forest honey is celebrated as the six-generation ancestor of the roast pigeon marinated in húng lìu, and is always served on six kinds of emerald-green leaves, vegetables unknown to all, never seen in any market. That six-vegetable salad is both sweet and refreshing, it just shoots down your throat without you even swallowing. That six-vegetable salad is a godsend to those with a chronic sore throat. Later I met six other schoolgirls named Yamina, with six younger brothers named Yasin. At the end of the year they all gave me six handkerchiefs, embroidered with six flowers and six leaves. But this Yamina is the one I remember most. Her mom's six pigeons spreading their wings on six kinds of emerald leaves is something that will always remain in my memory.

I'm Yellow

Hàng Cỏ station at midnight.

I'm waiting for my train. I only have a shirt on. My scarf and hat, sweater and outer coat are all in my duffel bag. I'm afraid that the train will pull into the station while I'm sleeping. I don't dare sit. I know I only need sit down on that step and I'll sleep like a baby. I don't go and check the timetable. Neither do I go and buy a ticket. I'm afraid that I'll still be at the ticket booth when the train guard blows his whistle. That the ticket fee has seen a fivefold increase in the last five years. That the Vietnamese currency has undergone a fiftyfold inflation since my paintings were taken away by the souvenir-hungry foreign visitors. That I will have to stand two hours in the ticket line. That I'll have a slip of the tongue and say I want a ticket not to Yên Viên but to Hà Nội, to Hàng Cỏ station. The ticket lady will reach for her microphone and call the guards. Eight guards will close in on me, my wrists will be forced into handcuffs, my body into a secured van, I will be carried body and cuffs to the mental hospital in Trâu Quỳ. The next day at eight p.m., after watching the arts and culture program on Hà Nội TV, Loan will get a phone call and bring my family and medical records to the director of the asylum. The hospital in Hà Nội has washed their hands of the crack in my skull, so the mental hospital doesn't have any reason to keep me. I will go home with Loan to be treated there. Everything will go back to how it was. The annulled contract will turn out to be effective still. Until when—I can't bear to think about that.

Loan hates the train. She says she doesn't want anything to do with the railway industry. When my paintings still hadn't found a place in the galleries, we only spent our days around Hà Nội. When my paintings went for fifty dollars each, Loan said we needed to go to the countryside for a round of the relatives. The relatives never said a word of reproach. The relatives still sent us premium lychees and mung bean cakes. But we needed to do the rounds all the same. She called two xe ôm to the town of Hải Dương. Two hours later, the two bike taxis stopped in front of her house. We went in, greeted her family of dozens, ate two bunches of premium lychees and two boxes of Golden Dragon mung bean cakes, and in the early afternoon hugged the drivers' backs all the way back to Hà Nội.

I traveled a lot in my bachelor days. North, South, Central, no place was too far, no accent too hard on my ears. A few dozen times a year I took my backpack and train hopped. I was friendly with all the ticket inspectors. They just bummed a few cigarettes from me, gave me a few pats on the shoulder, then left me to my own devices, I would sit if there was a spare seat, stand if there was none, retreat to the toilet if even standing was impossible, and if the toilets were locked I would go to the cooks, help them wash the dishes and clean the tables. Train hopping a few dozen times a year, I knew by face and name all the cooks in the railway industry. I met Loan in Hải Phòng. She was the last cook in the railway industry that I came to know the face and name of. I helped her wash the dishes and clean the tables on the train from Hải Phòng to Lạng Sơn. This one train hop cost me five whole years. At thirty-nine, I am now wary of all cooks in the railway industry, and of all women named Loan, every last one was once a cook in the railway industry.

I don't remember when I got on the train. Nor do I remember when that woman arrived, the woman sitting in the last row. There were still a few places left in the train car when I got on. People were eating and chatting up a storm. I found a corner by a window. For the last half a day I have been smoking. The smoke protected me from the smell of food, that reminder of all those meals Loan cooked during the last five years, all nutritious meals up to the standards of railway industry cooks. Most nutritious were those in the final fifty days, those dishes of who knows how many eggs, prepared by who knows what method, frying or stir-frying or boiling or putting into soup, but definitely up to standard, so definite it has been the only thing on the menu for my last hundred and fifty meals. I've got to smoke for another five days before I can be enticed to put my chopsticks into a bowl of rice again, another fifty days before I can touch eggs. Loan has very precise ways to punish me.

The woman sits looking out of the window. People are still eating and chatting up a storm. People are still coming and going as freely as if in a market. I thought she would have gone ages ago. I went to the next carriage for the toilet, stood in several lines, sneezed and spat several gobs of spit, and came back to find her still there. I put out my cigarette, went with the ticket inspector to visit the guard in his cabin, downed a few cups of rice wine, listened to some tattle and prattle. At Nam Định station I ran into a former buddy from our train-hopping circle. He's still hopping trains now but always with a few dozen cans of beer and a thermos of ice on him. Says he must provide for his wife and kids. After getting married, he took up hopping interprovincial buses as well. After the birth of his kids, he further took up hopping trucks and tourist buses. He says, boss you're really living the life. Our old days of carefree train hopping, now that was the life. When the train was about to move he jumped off, even more nimbly than five years ago. Five years ago, he train hopped fifteen times a year. Now in any given day there are fifteen trains passing through, fifty buses stopping by, and who knows how many trucks and tourist buses calling at the station of Nam Định.

I wandered through all cars, but gave the kitchen car a wide berth. The ticket inspector gave me a pat on the shoulder when he passed: being a son-in-law of the railway scarred you for life, eh.

The train arrives at Vinh at midnight. All passengers in the car are deep in slumber, adults leaning back in their seats, kids lying right on the floor. The city shimmers outside the window. I spent a week here once. Though I have no memory of it now. The word "memory" is enough to seal my eyes shut. The Twin Towers of Vinh, two five-story buildings erected by the Soviets, are the last thing I see before plunging into an endless sleep. Never have I slept so sweetly. Never have I woken so pleasantly. The woman seems to be moving her lips in greeting. I raise my hand and wave. I don't know why I did such a thing. The whole carriage is still deep in slumber. Turns out I only dozed for a bit. Turns out sleeping without Loan by my side is more pleasant than I could imagine. No one pays any heed to my wave. I repeat the gesture. Still without understanding why. The woman puts her hand on her chest, then points to mine. I shrug. I myself don't know where I will get off. She also shrugs. I look at her, wary. I remind myself that I have only tasted freedom for a little over a day.

I take out my cigarettes. Across the car she's moving her lips again. I ignore her. My guard is up. Even Loan was not so blatant on the first day. I smoke cigarette after cigarette. The other passengers raise their voices. A chorus of country folk spring up and tell me to go somewhere to off my suicidal self. I snub out my cigarette, put my towel back into my duffel bag, tie my shoelaces, and put on my hat. Again the other passengers raise their voices. They wish me luck on my journey. I wave a dismissive hand. Loan also wished me luck on my journey. The pro train hoppers never said such things. We avoided each other from the

91

first distant glimpse. The latecomer would automatically give up the train to the one who got on first. This law of the train-hopping circle is still remembered by my beer-peddling buddy. He had run some distance on the ground before he looked back and waved. I also raised my hand and waved. This was something we'd done on at least twelve previous occasions. I bumped into him every time I hopped the train to Nam Định. I gave it up when he got on first. He gave it up when I got on first. The law is very clear. Later I came to dub him the Nam Định fellow. The Nam Định fellow was the youngest of the whole pro train-hopping circle. Young and handsome. I'm much older than him. Maybe that's why he calls me boss.

The palest was the Ninh Bình fellow. His film star fair skin was augmented by his sunglasses and fedora. His presence on the platform would draw a host of girls to lean out the windows, enthusiastically waving their handkerchiefs. But with me already aboard, he wouldn't dare hop on. The stupefied girls would watch how he and I waved at one another as exuberantly as in some Soviet spy drama. His splendor rubbed off on me. Whenever the train was pulling into Ninh Bình station, I would smooth my hair and rearrange my outfit, ready for a sumptuous waving match.

The darkest was the Đồng Hới fellow. If the train passed by Đồng Hới at night it would be virtually impossible to see him. Tactfully, he would light a cigarette and stand at the door smoking.

The one I often ran into at Huế was tall and slim. We only hopped on at Huế if we couldn't hear his rhythmic guitar. "Diễm xưa" is the only song in ten years I ever heard him play. He only needed to clear his throat and all would be silenced. The ticket inspector would give him a pat on the shoulder when he passed: if there were several singers like you on every train our security staff could all put their feet up. Girl students often bought train tickets to get off at Huế. They would sit there listening to that song about a beauty of yore, steal a glance at his face, then meekly turn around and take the return train. Once I looked up from the platform to see the whole carriage had turned deep violet, as if the whole girls' school of Đồng Khánh had moved into the train. Then I looked to my right to see dozens of male students in white shirts and parted hair, leaning back against the trees to listen to the misty rain upon the ancient temple. He's the only one I didn't name after his station. To me he is always the *Diễm xưa* fellow. The song will always remind me of him.

The Nha Trang fellow was no less artistic. Also strumming his guitar days and nights. Also with a single-song repertoire. I didn't know if it was also by Trịnh Công Sơn, but it was also very emotional. From the platform I would always hear him crooning, *autumn's here again oh our beloved Nha Trang, passion in your smile and in your eyes, red flags flying over our brand-new life, the spacious winds of autumn, the far-sailing boats, the sea of ours sparkling on the horizon.* The passengers in the carriage clapped like thunder. The girls begged to be allowed to accompany him. He was no less artistic in a duet, he could maneuver any kind of voice, and complement them gracefully. Singing to his guitar, girls from the North would shy from high-pitched notes, those from the South would skip the low, those from the Central would try their best to enunciate every word. The ticket inspector gave both of us a pat on the shoulder when he passed: you should apply for the Railway song and dance troupe.

The Sài Gòn fellow was always in denim shirt and jeans, a pair of Thai flip-flops on his feet, a fat leather wallet straining the pocket at his buttocks. We set aside a few minutes for a proper handshake whenever we ran into one another. He called me Hà Nội boss. I called him Sài Gòn boss. If I offered him a Thủ Đô cig, he would surely whip out his lighter to light me one of his Triple-Fives. Once his packet came out empty, so he told me to wait and ran to the café next to the station, emerging after two minutes with a borrowed plastic tray bearing a still-sealed packet of 555s and two aromatic cups of Trung Nguyên coffee. I was uneasy. I told him not to call me Hà Nội boss. Hà Nội fellow, Northern bastard, water spinach muncher, yes-yes-but-actually-no bureaucrat, whatever he wanted to dub me, just not Hà Nội boss. He smiled and said nothing.

I asked why he chose to stick with the train hoppers. Again he smiled and said nothing. I voiced my suspicion that something was weighing on his heart. Still he smiled and said nothing. I didn't know how to proceed. We parted ways. Several months later, when we met again, it was Hà Nội boss and Sài Gòn boss once again.

I didn't forget the Thanh Hóa fellow either. He had a round face, short hair, and the air of an intellectual. The last time we met, I'd been occupying the train for a whole half day. He came up to me and said he knew the law, but it was too late to get on another train. His girlfriend was waiting for him at Vinh station. Their relationship was a secret to her family. Tomorrow they would board the train and head south. On tickets bought with real money. He'd had it up to here with hopping trains. His girlfriend had made him promise to retire for good. They would start a new life in the South. Also, he wanted to take this chance to say hello to me. Our paths had crossed so many times and yet we'd never exchanged a single word. He told me to drop by whenever I found myself in the South. But we would please talk only about happy things, no nostalgic stuff. He would be unhappy and his girlfriend would disapprove. She'd made him promise to forget his train-hopping past. He jumped off at Thanh Hóa station. From the platform he reached up to shake my hand a few times and say, boss, good luck on your journey. Then he laughed and said, you see, I'm now fully assimilated into my new life. He wanted to say more about his girlfriend but then the train started. He raised his hand and waved, saying, boss, good luck on your journey.

Loan didn't run away from her family for me. Neither did she make me promise to forget my train-hopping past. When we got home from the registry office she threw my backpack into an aluminum tub. And nonchalantly produced a can of gasoline. I didn't know when she'd found the time to buy it. Even our bicycles were borrowed, so of course we didn't have a motorbike. I tried to seize the can. I warned her of the fire hazard. After dozens of train hops a year I knew that every female cook in the railway industry gets disciplined for arson at least once. Every quarter year several carriages of the Thống Nhất would go up in flames, if not because of drought-induced forest fires then because of female cooks. Loan said that pest of a thing should be thrown away as fast as possible. She presently threw my backpack into the trash can as an example. Pest is how she described anything to do with my train-hopping past. My backpack, my worker's outfit, my toothbrush with its broken handle—these were all pests of things. Snoring, smoking, slurping instant noodles, bathing without soap, yawning without covering my mouth—these were all pests of habits. The ticket inspectors from the days of old were also dubbed those old pests. Those old pests are here to haunt us again. Those old pests spit tea leaves all over my floor. Those old pests burned my tablecloth with their thuốc lào pipes. Those old pests gave the kid a stale cake and her tummy growled all night. Those old pests pushed their muddy bikes into my home. Those old pests hung their stinking towels right beside my blouses. Those old pests went a week without a shower, walked through the door and dove right into the bed, under the sheets and began to snore like tractors.

Yesterday, when I left home, Loan said with a smile, going adventuring with your old pests again? Adventuring is a word she only uses between us. She presented me to her colleagues and acquaintances as an artist, a progeny of Hà Nội University of Fine Arts, an established name from numerous joint and solo exhibitions. The day we went to Hải Dương to do the rounds of her relatives she told them, a painting by my man buys a hundred kilograms of your premium lychees. To the journalist who came looking for a story for the seventieth anniversary of our university, Loan offered my paintings as the embodiment of the sublime kind of art in which academic learning and worldly experience are harmoniously intertwined. I don't know what else she said, but his article in the Lao Động the following day celebrated me as the truest artist who, with my top-notch degree in my backpack, traipsed my way into every nook and cranny of my beloved country. Not a trace of "adventure" or "train hopping" in the whole story. Loan said that was just the way advertising works. She said that other artists were even more sophisticated advertisers. They would sell a piece for two hundred dollars and advertise that they had just sent away a dozen at over a thousand each. They would get two paintings up on the wall next to twenty conical hats in some overseas shop specializing in such Southeast Asian hats, and advertise that they'd been signed for a solo exhibition at a world-renowned gallery. She said that normally 30 percent of your expenditure goes into just getting people to look at your stuff, art is the only industry where advertising is free. Loan was the first railway cook who branched out into art advertisement. She would become immortal. Every single calculation of hers was correct, every step a step toward immortality.

The woman is somehow standing right beside me.

I take out my cigarettes. The ticket inspector gives me a pat on the shoulder to ask for one, then another pat to wish me good luck on my journey. The train draws into a minor station. They announce that the train will stop for only thirty seconds. My feet hit the ground with a thud. Turns out my habits didn't get thrown out with my backpack. I lift my foot, ready to go. The woman makes surprised mewing sounds in her throat. She raises her hand and waves in my direction. She shuffles and shifts but doesn't dare jump. Other passengers crane their necks for a good look. One of the necks belongs to the inspector. No one makes a move. I can do nothing but turn back and stretch out my hand to her. My guard is still up. I remind myself that I've only tasted freedom for a little over a day.

She's now standing right next to me, asking if I'm going somewhere then can she come along. Turns out she can speak. She has a sullen face but her voice isn't so bad. She mixes three or four accents but it's not so bad. My guard is up alarmingly. Loan's voice was once as sweet as syrup. Later it became even more syrupy in front of journalists and gallery owners. She said that was also the way advertising works. I tell myself I must raise my guard even more. I shrug. I tell the woman that I myself don't know where I'm going, or even where this station is. She also shrugs. I'm furious. I turn and walk away.

She runs after me. She asks if I'm going somewhere then can she come along. The more she pleads, the more furious I become. I stub out my cig. I ask her if she knows what prison is. She nods. I tell her I've just walked out of prison. She nods. I say I just want to walk until my legs melt, to sleep whenever my eyelids meet, to smoke instead of eating, to yawn as much as I please without scrambling to cover my mouth, without smiles and sorrys and thank yous. She nods. I say I despise all rules. She nods. I say I hold all notions of politeness in contempt. She nods. I say there's nothing that bugs me more than being wished good luck on my journey. She nods. She seems to understand it all. I look down and continue on my way.

Again she runs after me. I act as if I don't hear her. I walk intently. Still she trots after me. Loan once trotted after me for a month. Now my guard is at its maximum height. I swear to myself I won't cede an inch. I walk a long way. Then a very long way. Then it becomes so long I lose all sense of distance.

The snaking road vanishes in blackness. I've lost count of the times I've walked like this. And of the times I've reminisced about such walking, over these last five years. Loan hates the train. She swears that she's done once and for all with the railway industry. She disapproves of all means of transport. Whether public or personal. The xe ôm trip to her hometown was the only time we went outside Hà Nội after getting married. Even later, when my paintings fetched a hundred dollars each thanks to her way of advertising, she never went anywhere. I never saw her father again after that trip. Her mother came to the hospital the day after Loan gave birth, she put two bunches of premium lychees on the table, held her new granddaughter for half an hour, and left. Loan made no comment. And I didn't ask her for one. Her mother came to visit once more. It was a year later. She gave the baby girl two boxes of Golden Dragon mung bean cakes, held her for half an hour, fed her half a bowl of rice with a spoon, and left again.

That was the last time I saw my mother-in-law. And no one else in Loan's family ever paid any visit. I suggested she take our daughter to

Hải Dương for a few days. So that the baby would know the taste of premium lychees. Loan said with a smile that we could wait until my paintings were priced at a thousand dollars each, then we could drive our own car there and bring back two baskets of lychees to nibble away.

I didn't know if that was a joke or not. I never knew if anything Loan said was a joke or not. She has a talent for saying things with a smile. She has a knack of putting people on edge. The gallery owners and journalists often found themselves on edge in her presence. She said that was also the way advertising works. I too was on edge when she said my paintings would one day fetch a thousand dollars each. She watched the art market in Vietnam as diligently as a Vietnamese businessman watches the global dollar market. Every Saturday, she would don a dress and sunglasses and do a round of the Hà Nội galleries. She called this marketing. Every Sunday she would spend half a day listing what I needed to paint in the coming week. She called this commissioning.

In the first few years, there were times when still lifes filled up our home, or Turtle Towers lined up in several rows, or abstracts vied with pots and pans in the kitchen, or sunset seas with fishermen's boats invaded the spaces under our bed, table, chairs, wardrobe, and cupboards.

The age of naivete passed like a dream, the same way Loan got up one morning, placed some calls to thirty cafés all over Hà Nội and in less than three hours succeeded in clearing out all still lifes, Turtle Towers, abstracts, and seascapes. The age of innocence also passed like a dream, my paintings began to find their way into middling galleries, to pop up in stories by middling journalists, to follow middling foreign tourists home to adorn their middling living rooms.

Monday mornings before going to work, Loan would make me a cup of coffee, then hand me the commission list she'd made the day before. For the last two years our contract had called for a painting every two days. My job was to produce. Her job was to translate the product into dollars.

For the last two years Loan has maintained a rate of 100 percent accuracy. She said the fifty Hội An Old Towns would move in three months, and on the ninety-first day we were assailed by phone calls from all the middling galleries. She said the Bình Trị Thiên tourist agency had just mandated that tourists all over the country be herded to gape at the freshly replaced bricks on the roof of King Thành Thái's library, and sure as not the hundred Afternoons in the Imperial Cities went straight to the airport, bypassing any wall. Loan said babies with lotuses were required in all kinds of variations, lotus in front, lotus in back, lotus on left, lotus on right, baby boy, baby girl, baby at three, five, seven, baby in short sleeves, baby in long sleeves, in patterns, in plain, I could do whatever, I could make up whatever, but I must produce fifty of them within a hundred days. I was alarmed. We didn't have room for fifty babies if they failed to leave the house. Loan said with a smile that her marketing had penetrated right into the municipal people's committee and sniffed out ten building permits for ten tourist hotels; her marketing judged that if each hotel adopted five babies, we were good.

One hundred days later, I was putting the finishing touches to the final baby's patterned shirt when a hotel van came by to pick up twenty baby girls aged from three to seven. One week later, another hotel phoned to ask for ten babies, either boy or girl, vivid or pastel, happy or sad. One month later, my daughter said with a long face that she had no friends left to play with.

Five years ago, when Loan was as clueless about the way of advertising as she was about marketing, I said she still had time to change her mind. She said with a smile that her journalist friend once judged that a painter's life is the easiest nowadays, even a real estate broker's or a private banker's is no match. After a pause, she again said with a smile that her typist friend who worked for BMW judged that the ritziest BMWs nowadays are registered to artists, even Politburo members and drug lords trail behind.

Last night, before I left for good, Loan said with a smile that they expected five times more foreign tourists would come to sail in Hạ Long Bay this summer, so the fifty paintings I'd produced in the last fifty days could be priced five times higher than the two-hundred-dollar market rate. To what extent those fifty paintings resemble the real bay is not something she concerns herself with, but they would help her take our daughter to Hải Dương for the rounds of the relatives. So that the baby would know the taste of premium lychees. Loan said I was wrong. She hates the train and detests the motorbike but a BMW is fine in her book. Never had she seen a bike crashing into a BMW, just the other way around. In the fifty days that I was up to my neck in Hạ Long Bays, she'd got her driving license, and her friend had picked for her a lime-green BMW with an automatic box. The license is only good for awing the traffic police, because her lime green BMW needs no maneuvering, it stops on its own at red lights, starts at green lights, back away at trucks and charges full speed at Dream bikes. The automatic box is the invention of the century. At the very moment that I stepped onto the Thống Nhất, she and her daughter were on a cyclo to go and try out the automatic box. She is the first railway cook to drive a BMW with an automatic box. She is the first Vietnamese to possess the invention of the century. She will become immortal. Every single calculation of hers is correct. Every step is a step toward immortality.

I heave my bag onto my shoulder, lamenting the backpack Loan threw away. I've walked a long way. I don't care how long. And I don't care where to. I just walk, fixedly. And stop at times to pinch my ears. It hurts. I sat for twelve hours on the train, Hàng Cỏ station is now twelve hours behind me. Even if Loan in her BMW chased after the Thống Nhất for twelve hours, she wouldn't guess that I'd get off at this station. She would surely visit the Twin Towers when she passed by Vinh. The Twin Towers would surely be holding a nationwide BMW exhibition, parading ten models with automatic boxes and ten artists representing the province of Nghệ An. Ten artworks of all kinds of media, oil and lacquer and watercolor and silk and ink wash and bamboo paper and shell inlay and carved wood and cast bronze and carved stone, all on the single theme of Lotus Village, the natal town of Uncle Hồ. The diasporadic Việt Kiều from Lotus Village would respectfully pay one million đồng for each of the ten works, then respectfully present their certificates from the Twin Towers of Vinh when going through customs, and no police would dare touch such works of art. Loan would whip out her mobile phone to consult her friend who'd not long ago opened a gallery on Tràng Tiền street. She would advise Loan to take the shell inlay painting and display it in her gallery at a 400 percent markup. The Việt Kiều from Lotus Village would stop by after visiting the Turtle Tower, respectfully pay with their foreign credit card, then respectfully wrap it up in foam and cotton wool, respectfully take it to a slow shipping service, and respectfully ask a family member to drive to Charles de Gaulle later and pick the package up, so that when Uncle Hồ's birthday comes around they could respectfully take it to the embassy as a gift, where the ambassadors would respectfully remove all the foam and cotton wool and hang it on two nails next to the other twenty shell inlays, all with a label underneath that reads, most respectfully, "Lotus Village."

This friend of Loan is a lawbreaker. She is close with this lawbreaker in the train-hopping circle. I ran into the fellow when I first started out. You could hear him way before you saw him. At Quảng Bình station you wouldn't need to look out of the window; you heard his booming voice and automatically made yourself scarce to cede the train to him. He was the only one who proudly broke the law; the official law was nothing to him, he declared, let alone this unspoken train-hopping law. Then one day he vanished into thin air. The whole circle breathed a sigh of relief. Last year when I put on a tie and dress shoes to escort Loan to her friend's gallery opening, guess who I saw. He too was in tie and shoes. He too saw me. Neither of us had said a word to the other when Loan called me aside. I'd better be social for once and strike up a conversation, she said. Here was a Việt Kiều from Germany who sought an investment opportunity in his home country. The whole cigarette smuggling operation in East Berlin answered to him. When, in the near future, the East Berliners inevitably swarmed West Berlin, his East Berlin cigarette smugglers would surely be among them. She said this man was no stranger to her. He once helped her clean tables and wash dishes. He once promised to secure her a job cleaning tables and washing dishes in East Berlin. But *this was a different time, you can't pick fights by dwelling on the past, you can't ruin things by clinging to old promises. She said if I couldn't find it in me to be social, she would. I stood in a corner, listening to his booming voice. After a while, all the guests automatically made themselves scarce to cede the whole gallery to him.*

Loan's friend bore the Quảng Bình fellow no grudge. A year after the fall of the Wall, when the West Germans helped the East Germans smash up a million coal fireplaces, she left the Lauchhammer coal factory, itself slated for a visit from some West German bulldozer. Her plan was to fly home and continue her service at the Quảng Ninh coal factory. She met him at the airport. He tore up her ticket and threw away the few nude stockings and chocolate bars she had with her. He told her not to cry over such pests of things. He told her to come with him. I came with him alright, she told me, I cleaned the tables and washed the dishes for his East Berlin cigarette smuggling operation. Sometimes I cleaned corpses. It was scary. After ten years, I told him I wanted to retire. He made me promise to never again have anything to do with the coal or Quảng Ninh. He said he would never go back to Quảng Bình either. If we were to look for one another later on, it'd be in either Hà Nội or Berlin. He paid me some tens of thousands of deutsche marks for all my years cleaning tables and washing dishes. He gave me tens of thousands more as a bonus for all the corpses I'd cleaned. He said a hundred thousand plus was nothing to him. Even several million was nothing. Breaking the law in Vietnam got him a modest piece of rice paddy. Breaking the law in the united Germany got him accounts in the top Swiss banks. Success comes only to the lawbreakers. I heeded his words, she said, so I stayed in Hà Nội. I heeded his words, so my gallery is the only one that breaks the law. The Hà Nội art market put all its eggs into selling Hạ Long Bays and self-portraits to tourists. I fill half my gallery with Hạ Long Bays and self-portraits, but the other half with shell inlays to quench the thirst of homesick Việt Kiều. Only shell inlays will do for the Việt Kiều. Mother with baby, Tai girl in ethnic attire, young lady of Hà Nội, fawn at a spring, One Pillar Pagoda, Tràng Tiền bridge, Bến Thành market, child hero-saint Gióng ascending to heaven, the two Trưng sister-generals on their war elephants, Hưng Đạo Vương and his glorious battle on the Bạch Đằng river ... whether the subject is traditional or modern, it must be rendered in shell inlay. The more shell inlaid, the happier the Việt Kiều. On the way to the airport he had reiterated over and over again, success comes only to the lawbreakers. It's the truth. This lawbreaking truth will be etched into my mind until the day I die.

The snaking road vanishes into blackness. I clearly hear footsteps behind me. I don't need to look back to know it's the woman. I take out my cigarettes. I remind myself that I have only tasted freedom for a little over a day. I shake my bag. No clanging sound. I open the flap, reach all the way inside, and rummage for a while, but my toothbrush and toothpaste are its only contents. The key is now secure in some gutter. Reassured, I go on. And stop at times to pinch my ears. It hurts. I walk purposefully. And mentally list the twenty-nine train-hopping buddies as I walk. I wonder where all of them have drifted to now. Whether any of them is a more hardworking provider than the Nam Định fellow, or a bolder lawbreaker than the Quảng Bình fellow. Whether I would have bumped into the Sài Gòn boss if I'd gone all the way to Bình Triệu station. For the last five years I've smoked only one brand, the Thủ Đô. Loan always had a packet of 555s in her bag, only taking it out for journalists and gallery owners. She said that was the way advertising works. Thanks to her advertising, I had a few chances to enjoy the taste of a 555. Those few times weren't enough to help me tell an authentic cig from one made in Chợ Lớn, but enough to make me nostalgic for the Sài Gòn fellow. Enough to make me figure out that he, too, always had a packet in his bag, only taking it out for bosses. Apparently the way of advertising was already practiced all over the country even back then. Those few times were enough to make me wonder why little old me deserved him practicing the way of advertising on me. Why little shabby Hà Nội deserved Sài Gòn practicing the way of advertising on it. He was so polite that he called me boss. He was so polite that he overlooked my inane questions. He was so polite that he just looked at me, smiled, and said nothing. The Hanoian may be polite, but the Saigonese is ten times more so. I could hop trains for tens of years more and I would never understand the politeness of the Vietnamese.

Last night, before I left, Loan said with a smile that five years of living in Hà Nội had taught her how to be as polite as a Hanoian. It's one thing to be mild-mannered and soft-spoken, to be always ready with your thank yous and sorrys, to remember your greetings when coming and leaving, to crack a smile every few minutes, but it's a whole other level to feign obliviousness, to act as if nothing whatsoever has happened. That ability manifests only in those possessing a five-year-plus Hà Nội citizenship, Loan said. She said country folk are always quick to air their opinions, they offend people the second they open their big mouths and then brag about it, honest me ain't play no games, my thoughts just go out without no filter. She said we two should split up as politely as bona fide citizens of the capital, we should act as if nothing whatsoever had happened. I could take up adventuring with those old pests as I pleased. She would inform the middling galleries that I was going into retreat for a while. Finding a backwater plot to construct a palace for the arts being all the rage among Hanoian artists nowadays, no brow would be raised at my retreat. I could keep on adventuring with those pro train hoppers as I pleased. She would hire a fifth-year student from the University of Fine Arts to replicate my fifty best sellers, and her marketing research would decree the number of clones made from them. She had photos of them all, negative and positive. She assured me that the galleries wouldn't know the difference, the customers wouldn't doubt the result, the middling journalists wouldn't question the practice. All it takes is for me to act like a bona fide Hanoian, as if nothing whatsoever had happened.

The river is not wide enough, the water not clear enough, and I am not brave enough to swim to the other side. I don't know when the woman caught up to walk beside me. She asks if I'm going somewhere then can she come along. The more she pleads, the more furious I become. I stub out my cig. I ask her if she knows that I myself don't know *where I am going. She says that all the towns from north to south, Ninh Bình or Thanh Hóa, Vinh or Đồng Hới, Tam Kỳ or Quảng Ngãi, Quy Nhơn or Phan Thiết, are mine to choose from.*

So she does know quite a few stations. She has a sullen face but her voice isn't so bad. I ask if she would go with me if I now take a bus all the way to Buôn Mê Thuột, and from there all the way up to Đắc Lắc. She swears she would never complain of carsickness.

I ask if she could stick it out for a whole month or a whole year. She says she would follow me for the whole month or the whole year. Airplane or train, ship or bus, even xe ôm, she would never ask for a barf bag or a sickness pill.

She mixes three or four accents in her voice, but it's not so bad. I'm afraid she might once have washed dishes and cleaned tables in the railway industry. I ask about her employment history. She says her job is to be an ideal companion.

I ask about her cuisine history. She rattles off seventeen years of sweet catjang soup and rice pot–steamed pig brains in Hà Nội, five years of cabbage with mutton in Leningrad State University cafeteria, another ten years of instant noodles for breakfast and sandwiches for lunch and a choice one or the other for dinner in Paris and the surrounding areas. Even I can't compete with a CV like that. One look at a pig brain steamed in a rice pot, no matter whether normal rice or sticky, cooked in a cast-iron pot or electric, and I'll vomit my guts out. Cabbage and instant noodles I have neither love nor hate for, but if I ever train hop my way to Leningrad or Paris, I'll surely shell out for black caviar and foie gras, and break my baguette into halves, one to eat right away while it's still crusty, the other to wrap in newspaper to put in my duffel bag and save for the following morning when the train arrives in London. A London baguette could buy three in France, which means three hundred in Vietnam.

I tell myself not to let my guard down. Her cuisine CV is truly unrivaled, but artists aren't the only ones with exceptional self-advertising skills. I ask about comfort. She says I need only be concerned for myself.

Her extensive training has left her able to nod off for the three commuting hours every day, whether in the drowsiest lulls or in the middle of the most dramatic train or bus transfers. And she's no stranger to power loss in the middle of a meal, hot water loss in the middle of a shower, heaters giving up the ghost in the middle of a subzero night.

I eye her with suspicion. I was once in Đồng Hới. I know why the Đồng Hới fellow was the darkest of us thirty pro train hoppers. But subzero temperatures are beyond me. How could she fall asleep in the freezer compartment. I ask her who she is and why she thinks I should trust her. She says that I will find that she has no talents to speak of, only the talent of being the easiest companion ever.

I tell her she'd better lay down her conditions. She says we can go anywhere I please, as long as it's not Chợ Lớn. I shrug. I have no reason to go to Chợ Lớn. She says I can do anything I like but not turn myself into thụy. I ask what thụy is. She says thụy is the mystery to end all mysteries. Not until her last breath will she be able to understand thụy. I shrug. I could live to a hundred and there would still be a multitude of things I won't understand.

The river isn't wide enough. The water isn't clear enough. I'm not brave enough to swim to the other bank. She asks if I go somewhere may she come along. She pleads so insistently. She has a sullen face but her voice is not so bad. I pull out my cigarettes.

We take a boat, then we walk for another day, two days, another week, then for how long I don't know. I don't feel it necessary to know. And she doesn't ask. So many days pass without a word between us. We walk intently. Walk by day and rest at night. Rivers are left behind. Forests are left behind. Hà Nội is completely and utterly left behind.

Four p.m. on a Sunday. The guy called. He asked why Vĩnh hadn't been over to see Paul and Arthur for a while. I could think of no explanation. Then, he said, write what you like but please leave people you know out of it. Your friends back in the country are all taking issue with your *Made in Vietnam*. Your best friend called your parents in tears, what a good friend you are to describe her in such words, you spelled out her very name and her place of work, you spun a thousand fantastical yarns, now she's terrified to show your book to anyone, most of all her own husband, she's afraid even he will get the wrong end of the stick. Your next-door neighbor, director of institute whatsitsname, he stormed into your house, he yelled at your parents, doesn't their layabout of a daughter have anything better to do in France than make up stories about the speech he gave on TV, now everyone in the institute laughs behind their hands when they see him. He threatened to have you sued. He threatened to have your publisher sued. He said only capitalism is helpless against these rascal authors, only capitalism has their hands tied when it comes to their rogue's freedom. He would prove the superiority of socialism. This wasn't news to me. My parents had told me long ago. They'd had to apologize to my best friend and promise my neighbor the director that they would talk some sense into me. And they were true to their word. They told me that if I have that much time on my hands I should go ahead and defend my thesis. When the defense is done, if there's still time, I bring the guy back to Vietnam with me and do the rounds of the relatives, and show off my new diploma while we're at it. Such killing two birds with one joyous stone would be most meaningful. Having such a wedding would be most meaningful. Now that you can find a photocopy shop on every street, my parents would be willing to stand from morning till night to multiply my thesis into hundreds of copies. Every wedding invitation would go forth with a copy. The three-hour reception at the hotel would be more than enough time for me to present my research; I can just bring home my black gown and black mortarboard to wear to the wedding, no need to be wasteful by getting a new white áo dài and white veil. And the organizers wouldn't need to be wasteful by hiring a band, an MC, a greeter of guests. The guests would also be pleased; not only can they gorge themselves on champagne and cake, but also take home a chunky doorstop of French postgraduate learning; the next day when the professors and doctors of Hà Nội begin to peruse the first page, some fiery debates would be sure to explode, so fiery they'll ask Vietnam's online newspapers to step in as arbiters, and said newspapers will spend a whole month engaging in a heated competition to churn out commentaries on my French postgraduate thesis. My wedding to the guy would be the hottest news on all mass media channels. Everywhere people would be singing the praises of the newlyweds who are comrades in the pursuit of knowledge. My parents' thirty-nine years of sacrifice would be recognized by readers nationwide and acclaimed by the party and the government. Relatives, colleagues, friends, at any gathering, would eagerly inform one another about the most special, most intellectual wedding in Hà Nội. I didn't dare read to the end. The audacity of my parents' imagination astonishes me more and more with every passing day. My parents deserve a place in several other books. I told the guy, how about you tell me some Rennes anecdotes and I'll try starting a new novel. He said thanks but no thanks, he too dreads becoming a character of mine. He's afraid that I will spin a thousand fantastical yarns, spelling out his name and place of work for anyone to read. I didn't spare my parents or my best friend or my neighbor the director, so why should I spare him. He is a child of capitalism, he knows how to sue me and my publisher. Next summer when he has just deposited himself in front of my house in Hà Nội, when my father has not yet carried his bicycle upstairs and my mother not yet made him some lemonade, some random fellow will run up to him and enthusiastically ask why he isn't wearing his black suit and black tie, where he left his white car, why he hasn't sent out the wedding invitation together with his bride-to-be's postgraduate thesis. And it won't stop there, when summer comes I will have even more time on my hands, who knows if I won't attempt to translate my own book, a minor publisher hunting for some Southeast Asian names for their collection might take the risk and greenlight it, print a few hundreds of copies and sell it in the Métro station. His colleagues need something to distract their eyes, to cope with bouts of drowsiness in their three hours a day on public transport. At least one of his hundred colleagues will chance upon my book. Flicking through page after page teeming with identical Vietnamese names, their eyes would stumble across a French name, they would stop, they would read, they would reach for their mobile phone to inform another colleague. This other colleague would jolt awake from their own bout of drowsiness, and reach for their own mobile phone to inform another colleague again. An hour later when he is barely out of the Métro station, fifty of his colleagues would pounce on him, so it's true you went to Vietnam twelve times, so it's true you went from north to south, so it's true you went on a Soviet motorbike, so it's true you know all the telephone operators. He won't have found the words to correct them when the other fifty colleagues pipe up, you two both left a marriage behind, that's alright, that's all the better, you can better understand each other, one shouldn't get hung up on details. You two had better make it official, move in together, it won't be a family without husband and wife, children won't be happy without mom and dad. He broke into a cold sweat. He advised me to spare him this time. He said my charity is narrower than a needle's eye, not even a single thread can pass through it. He was convinced that Phượng's parents must be modeled after mine. It was so mean when you describe how the old dears are so afraid of breathing in water they take showers together in their newfangled bathroom, he said. I chortled. I didn't remember that detail myself—if only my parents would do such a lovely thing as taking a shower together. He said, you can spin whatever yarn you like but don't skimp on the paragraph breaks, your readers need to catch their breath, and don't forget a chapter break every few pages so they can practice counting to ten. I chortled. I hadn't expected my readers to have such exacting demands. He said, you can spin whatever yarn you like but don't let the critics force the dissident's hat on you, wearing that hat you won't be able to come back and see your parents. I chortled. I hadn't thought that the critics would be as quick-witted as the Home Office's counterespionage committee. He said, you can have the protagonist of *I'm Yellow* go from north to south as many times as you like, only don't rent him a Soviet bike, don't turn me into him, I advise you to spare me this time. I chortled. I'd had my eyes on this or that acquaintance to put into my books, but never thought about him. Then I was startled. How could he be reading my new novel already? I hadn't even finished it yet. I hadn't even sent a draft to my publisher. Hao Peng had told Vĩnh all about Beijing's ingenuity. In the year 2000 Beijing produced a bigender virus that can worm its way into anything. They multiplied it into a billion copies and slipped these into a billion computers inside and outside China. Seizing dozens of computers a month that propagandize for freedom and democracy, pluralism and multipartyism, Beijing has recently won the Reporters Without Borders Award for Internet Suppression. Maybe the guy is working for Beijing. Maybe Beijing knows I'm an Âu, so they tasked him with slipping a virus into my computer. Or maybe at some point during his twelve north-to-south Soviet-bike trips he became a counterespionage agent for Hà Nội. Hà Nội recently bought a Y2K bigender virus from Beijing, multiplied it into eighty million copies, and slipped these into eighty million computers inside and outside of Vietnam. I haven't shown any signs yet, I have only spun fantastical yarns, but his duty is to ensure that I am watched closely. He's read everything I've written. He remembers details I myself forget. He criticizes my style. He even puts ideas into my head. His asking me to run three laps around Belleville park every Sunday must be in order to check up on me. Dropping by my parents' house in Hà Nội each year can't be because my father carries his bicycle upstairs with more dexterity than any other host, or because my mother is more generous with sugar and ice than the city's thousands of iced lemonade stands. I told myself that I must keep my guard up around him. I changed the subject. Changing the subject is my forte. I said, I saw on television that your Rennes is home to a gargantuan university, where students spend all their days protesting, and teachers even cheer them on, students and teachers alike are tough nuts to crack, the right are wary of them, the left no less so. He lit up immediately, I spent four years as a student there. The best four years of my life. I met Hélène on the very first day. After two months we got engaged, after two years we got Paul, after two years again we got Arthur. We took turns marching in the streets to protest the government, took turns going to class, to the library, taking care of the kids, shopping for groceries, preparing meals, cleaning the house. At our diploma ceremony she carried the baby and I the toddler. She would wait outside my job interviews and I would wait outside hers, the baby in our arms, the toddler standing by. When Paul was two years old and Arthur three months, all four of us lay on the ground right in front of the university, to demand that the minister of education be fired. Students from the whole university lined up to bring milk and diapers for Arthur, water and toys for Paul. Many TV stations wanted to interview us, many newspapers sought stories. But Hélène and I only agreed to talk to the local outlets. By noon our family portrait was splashed over the front of *Le Monde*. In the afternoon the police had to take us home in their car. Hélène and I hugged each other and laughed like crazy. The uncomprehending kids also laughed like crazy. The guy just couldn't be stopped. His words poured out in a torrent. I suspected that if I listened to his intimate memories now, I would later have to tell him mine, so that he could compose his three-page report to Beijing. But he had become excited. He was caught up in his own flow. We lived together for another two years, then we took each other to court. Hélène said I snored too loudly, smoked too much, bathed without soap, sneezed without covering my nose or apologizing to those around me. She demanded that I quit all such habits. The court decreed two years of probation but she wouldn't accept anything longer than six months. In the seventh month she moved out. Taking only a small suitcase. Leaving no address. The kids and I were left behind in our apartment. The cat was left behind too. When the year was up, I went to the court but I found myself alone. Hélène didn't show up. I waited until it was pitch-dark outside but she didn't show up. They said it had to be rescheduled. They decided on another date. The second time, I was stood up again. They decided on yet another date. At the third strike, we were out. Now the case was closed for good. I didn't know where she was. The kids and I packed up and moved to Paris. My parents wept for a whole month, who do you know up there, where can you stay. Our apartment went back to the landlord. I'd found it in the ads at the dorm. The landlord had looked for a student tenant. Ideally one who was married with children and settled in a respectable life. I spent half a day cleaning that apartment before going to the maternity ward to bring Hélène and Paul home. The apartment had three bedrooms. Hélène said the second was for Paul and the last one would go to his younger sibling. When Arthur was born, she said the second was for the two of them and the last one would go to their younger sibling. During the years we lived there, the last room was always left unoccupied. Later I went to the library to see what Freud had to say. Freud told me that Hélène had a phobia of giving birth. People are obsessed with what they fear. Hélène when carrying Paul was already thinking of Arthur, and when carrying Arthur was already thinking of her next child. In the six years she stayed with me she prepared enough clothes and sundries for six babies. The third room was always left unoccupied but she still worried about where we'd put the next four kids. The more Freud explained, the more I felt for her. I didn't know where she was. I didn't ask my in-laws. I didn't tell Paul and Arthur to ask their grandparents. At first the old dears called a lot, crying every time and bombarding me with questions, did the three of us put up a Christmas tree, did we go sunbathing in the summer holidays, who was there to help out when both kids got a sore throat, did I know to buy them birthday cakes to take to school, so their teachers could stick candles in for them to blow out. I guess the old dears didn't know where she was either. I guess they wanted to ask me too. Anything Hélène had ever touched, I kept with me. Her slippers, her towel, her half-empty shampoo bottle, her never-opened powder jar, her lipstick worn down to the nub, her perfume bottle almost used up, I put all in a box; her clothing that had gone out of fashion, her winter boots, her textbooks, her postcards from years ago, I put in another four boxes. I kept the five numbered boxes beside my bed, and then beside my new bed in Paris. In the first months after she left, there was something in the mailbox addressed to her every day. Then the mail grew more sparse. Then no one wrote to Hélène anymore. Not even advertisers. Now the mailbox only ever contains catalogs addressed to the three of us, hawking men's shoes, men's socks, men's boxers, men's cologne, men's mani-pedis, barber services, Viagra, cigars, condoms, motorcycles with big engines. For the last twelve years I've been afraid that Hélène would come back at some point when the three of us are out. Once, back in Rennes, I came home to the cat lying in a corner with a full belly. I'd been at the office for the past ten hours, Paul at his kindergarten, Arthur at his nursery, so who had come in and fed it. I called my parents. I knocked at the next-door lady's. I went downstairs to ask the doorman. I crossed the street to ring the house opposite. I had my suspicions. Hélène was always so fond of the cat. She'd bought it on the day of our engagement. Coming home in the evenings, she would always feed the cat before preparing our dinner. For the last twelve years I've been afraid that she would knock on our door for thirty minutes without anyone being there to answer. She was always scared of being left outside. She was always scared of being left alone. In our six years together I never left her home alone for more than a day. My first job after graduation called for frequent trips to other provinces. Once I drove the whole night to be with her at home. Anxiously I imagined her lying hugging the cat and crying, and uncomprehending Paul and Arthur crying with her, mother and sons and cat crying till morning. Since the day she left, I often dream of her lying there crying in her new apartment, wherever that might be, cat on one side, six babies on the other. I go to the library to see what Freud has to say. Freud tells me that she was bitten by a cat as a child. People are obsessed with what they fear. Immediately after moving in with me she got a cat as companion. She spoiled us rotten but she spoiled the cat tenfold. Six such years wore her out. She left me and the cat and the two kids behind. The more Freud explains, the more I feel for her. I don't know where she is now. For the last twelve years I've had the names of all three of us listed in the phone book, so we'll be easy to find just in case. Our answering machine kicks in after the third ring. On each of my trips to Vietnam on holiday I call to check it every week. But Hélène never calls. Not once in twelve years. I don't care where she is now, or who she's with. I just want to see her. To ask why she never calls. Not once in the whole twelve years. None of my friends ever mention her now. They have each gone through a few marriages, finalized a few divorces, moved to a few new cities. They can't remember every tidbit from my past. Their children assume Paul and Arthur are adopted. Our neighbors eye us suspiciously. In the cinema, at the beach, in the supermarket, outside the school, in the basement garage, they all eye us suspiciously. For a whole month there's been a great fuss on TV about how gay people are claiming marriage and adoption rights. Paul says he doesn't want to go out with me anymore. Arthur says he prefers to stay with his brother. They too have forgotten Hélène. They say that at thirty-nine if I still run three laps around Belleville park every week, I could find a wife as easy as pie. They say I'd better find a wife soon and spare them the concern, and throw away those five boxes to spare the room a little space. They say I should forget in order to live. It's the truth. Forget in order to live. I go to the library to see what Freud has to say. Freud tells me that I was afraid of losing Hélène. People are obsessed with what they fear. For the six years I lived with her I always imagined the moment she would go away. For the six years I lived with her I always waited for the court. The more Freud explains, the more I feel for her. And there, finally, the guy stopped. I wondered if I should tell him that his life story was touching, his love story precious, his Hélène quite a character, his Freud a clairvoyant, I just didn't know if I'd ever have the talent to put them into a novel. He doesn't want to become my character, but even if he offered himself right now I could only turn him down. At last all I said was, turns out we're the same age, turns out you two also separated twelve years ago, turns out you moved to Paris at the same time I did, it's ten years already, time is as fast as a rocket. He said nothing. I said, I think Hélène is a beautiful name. He said nothing. I guess she must have the bluest eyes. He said nothing. I said goodbye. When I hung up, I realized that I hadn't asked him if we were going to run three laps around Belleville park next Sunday. Next Sunday is Vĩnh's birthday. Thụy promised he would call the boy on his twelfth birthday. Vĩnh has told me that he doesn't want anyone over, not even his friend Hao

Peng. He will rise early and plant himself by the phone and wait from dawn till dusk. Chợ Lớn by night is even more vibrant than by day. At night is when they sign their contracts, eat at their restaurants, swirl in their dance halls, push their mah-jongg tiles. And when they take their photographs. The black-and-white photograph that lets me gaze at Thụy. And Vĩnh at the pair of lanterns. He says the pair of lanterns burn scarlet. Every house in Chợ Lớn boasts a pair of scarlet-burning lanterns. Chợ Lớn isn't afraid that the hydroelectric plant at Trị An will one day run out of steam. War, union, sanction, đổi mới, they gladly leave such things to Hà Nội and Sài Gòn. Hà Nội and Sài Gòn managed to reach the Geneva Agreements after several million lives lost, the Paris Accord after another several million lives lost over eighteen years. In those eighteen years Chợ Lớn signed eighteen thousand contracts, and gave new lives to eighteen million ethnically Chinese Vietnamese. Chợ Lớn gladly leaves the running of national politics to Hà Nội and Sài Gòn. Chợ Lớn sits in a corner of District Five to orchestrate the national economy. Vĩnh gets worked up when he talks about Chợ Lớn. He says Chợ Lớn is the most important Chinatown in all of Asia, Chợ Lớn reigns supreme over the Chinatowns of Laos, Cambodia, Thailand, Nepal, Myanmar, Indonesia, Malaysia, South Korea, or Japan. He asks me why I didn't get on the train to Chợ Lớn that year, if I had then he wouldn't have to go and learn Chinese in rue Tolbiac, where he's spent five years to still be outstripped by Hao Peng, who spent five months babbling in a Hangzhou nursery. I don't know what to say. I have never told him about how Thụy left. I spin a lot of yarns about other people but I didn't dare tell Vĩnh about how Thụy left. Vĩnh says nothing more. At twelve he already knows when to stop. He doesn't ask if I will talk to Thụy on the phone next Sunday. In his mind, Thụy and I are two separate entities. I am his present, Thụy is his future. I am his mother, Thụy is his father, no need to mix up the two. I am France and Thụy is Chinatown. I am the departure point and Thụy is the destination. I am the three roast pigeons marinated in húng lìu for Sunday lunch, the vine spinach and jute soup for his sore throat, the secondary school where every year he has to advance a grade, the weekly two-hour Chinese class in rue Tolbiac, the kung fu class where three shifus teach fifteen disciples and a new belt must be conquered every quarter year. Thụy is the parachute into Baghdad in six years, the role of Tai Feng JSC's Gulf branch representative, the two thousand ethnically Chinese communities, the nation without borders, the sum of Paris and London and New York. My childhood was a gigantic family portrait. At twelve, Vĩnh understands that his father and mother are separate entities. My childhood was glasses of sweet catjang soup boiled with government-store candies, pig brains steamed in rice pots, tens and praise in my school reports. At twelve, Vĩnh knows that Tạ Hiện roast pigeon is best, that Chinese passports will be golden in six years' time. My childhood knew not a moment for personal hobbies. At twelve, Vĩnh deliberates over his father and mother. He takes care not to speak to me about Thụy. I suspect that he also takes care not to speak to Thụy about me. I don't know which is better, my childhood or his, or who is the more fortunate, him or me. During his years in nursery and then in kindergarten, Vĩnh only knew his father from a black-and-white photograph. Back then he never mentioned Thụy. And never asked about Chợ Lớn. It all began when I sent him to Chinese classes. It all culminated when I bought him a ticket to Vietnam, to go for a summer holiday. That September the first when I met him at the airport, it was like meeting Thụy of twenty-three years ago. His hair was cropped, his eyes were slanted. When night came, I took my things to go sleep on the sofa. Next Sunday, Thụy will call Vĩnh. He will dial my number, the only number I've had since moving to France. Or maybe he will come to France in person. After all, why not. Chợ Lớn reigns supreme among all the Chinatowns of

Asia. This is the twenty-first century, and Chợ Lớn wants to expand to new territories. Chợ Lớn is shrewder than the US or Bruxelles. While the US is busy fighting over oil wells in the Gulf, and Bruxelles has its hands full helping ten European governments convert to the euro, Chợ Lớn will be the first to breach the walls of post-Soviet Russia, which after nearly a century as the big brother of the socialist bloc now has to trade its diamonds and Sputniks for cabbage and mutton to fill their bellies, Heineken and vodka to wet their throats. Chợ Lớn sends Thụy to Paris to study the 13th arrondissement so they can design another hundred and thirty 13th arrondissements for the more than seventeen million square meters of the largest country in the world, stretching corner to corner from Europe to Asia, the Baltic to the Pacific. Next Sunday, Thụy will tell Vĩnh to come and meet him at Charles de Gaulle. Vĩnh will set his alarm for four a.m. but scramble out of bed when it's not even three. He will ask Hao Peng to go with him. Each will carry a bouquet. They'll take a taxi to the airport. Then go in and find Thụy, help him get his luggage, and take the same taxi back to Paris. Thụy will stay at The East Is Red, a hotel in the heart of Belleville. Vĩnh will ask for two weeks' absence from school. His homeroom teacher will consult with the headmaster. After taking all afternoon to discuss, they will agree that the boy's request has merit. He will accompany Thụy to the 13th arrondissement by bus every day. Father on a weekly ticket, son on a monthly. Father carrying his briefcase, son his backpack. Father in a suit and tie, son in immaculate white shirt and black pants. If Thụy can find no photo for his ticket, Vĩnh will take him to an automated photo booth. Insert four one-euro coins. And wait a few minutes for the four 3 × 4 cm portraits. Vĩnh will remind Thụy to sign his ticket or else the inspector will give him a twofold fine, and he can't even claim he has left his wallet at home because then the police would be called, the police here know how to deal with anything, they'd be more than willing to escort him home, flip over his mattress, open his drawers to hunt for the forgotten wallet. Vĩnh won't want the grumbling hotel employees to have to rearrange the mattress and fix the drawers, so he himself will check the photo and signature on Thụy's weekly ticket, then carefully put both tickets into a pocket in his boxers, where they'll be safe from even the most seasoned Parisian pickpockets. During their twice-a-day sixty minutes on the bus, Vĩnh will have ample opportunity to point out to Thụy the most celebrated Chinese restaurant in Belleville, famous for having served President Mitterrand on three separate occasions, each time three roast pigeons marinated in húng lìu and three plates of crispy duck skin. When the bus crosses the Place de la République, he will surely tell Thụy that this is where the French love to have their demonstrations. Last year his school was closed for the whole of May and June due to the teachers' strikes. He didn't know if I'd wanted to join them, he told me, but the two of us are on the same residence card, which expired in a few days. If I was detained then who would take our documents to the Cité and pay the fifty euros for the right to stay another eleven months and twenty-nine days. Right on the Place de la République, he will make sure to show Thụy a very handsome old building, the Tati supermarket, where they import socks, T-shirts, wool hats, cotton face towels, Eiffel Towers, canvas shoes, a million each annually and all Asian products, to sell to Asian tourists as souvenirs for their Asian families. His grandmother once came to Paris for a week, for a meeting with the Tai Feng branch representatives. She also spent a day in Tati and ended up with a tie for his grandfather to wrap around his neck in winter to avoid a sore throat, and an aluminum Eiffel Tower key ring for his car key so he won't have to keep having mechanics force the door open like he did thirty times in the last three years. A kilometer away from the square, between the 3rd and 2nd arrondissements, Vĩnh will plead with the driver to slow down a bit, so Thụy can see the tiny Chinatown where Hao Peng's fellow villagers from Hangzhou live. The travel agencies weren't as attentive as they should have been, Hao Peng said, they bought his fellow villagers tickets to Charles de Gaulle but forgot to have someone line up for a few residence cards in the Cité, and now his fellow villagers live their whole French lives in basements, only daring emerge to practice their Taijiquan at night. And the garment companies weren't as attentive as they should have been, they carried sewing machines to his fellow villagers in their basements to help them pedal their drowsiness away but they forgot to gift a few sequined dresses to the door ladies, who now phone the police every month without fail to suggest they send some cars to take his fifty fellow villagers to the airport. Only Beijing can be relied upon to be as attentive as they should. Beijing even signed a joint execution plan with the French Republic's Ministry of the Interior. The Ministry's work ends when Hao Peng's fellow villagers are seen off at the airport; after the plane takes off, the rest is on Beijing. Beijing will send air-conditioned tourist buses to the very door of the plane, load everyone's luggage, give each person a roast pigeon and a bottle of Coca-Cola, and drive non-stop to the very gate of their village in Hangzhou, then wait to see that everybody is inside with their door closed before heading back to Beijing. There is a myriad of things Vĩnh will want to show his father. Here is Le Phénix bookstore on the Boulevard de Sébastopol, where, when he comes to buy Mandarin textbooks, the shop assistant always asks for news from Chợ Lớn. Here is the Châtelet, the center of Paris, where most of the cinemas are, even a rather tiny one that shows original Chinese movies, where once he and Hao Peng got in to see Jackie Chan with the aid of drawn-on moustaches, glasses, and walking canes, and the ticket lady even asked, will you two old timers be able to see the screen. Here are the quays of the Seine where they sell nothing but used books, where a long time ago he found a notebook full of Chinese words, with such beautiful handwriting and for only three francs. He took it home and put it on his desk, and opened it from time to time, but after five years all he can understand are the days of the week, and some few proper names of places and people. Here is the Élisabeth stadium, where his kung fu class performed last year and I cheered so enthusiastically my glasses fell off, so after the show we dived under the seats to search and he had to skip the after-party to take me home. On the Métro he said he would stay at home the day after to take me to work. In the evening I opened my bag to put in my two sandwiches for lunch and the glasses were right there. We hugged each other and laughed like crazy. After that, whenever my glasses went missing, we both would rush to check my bag first. Thụy will surely laugh at this part and Vĩnh, elated, will surely dip back into his ten-year store of anecdotes to regale his father with. He will fall silent only when the bus enters the 13th arrondissement. He knows Thụy won't need his tour guiding now. Here Thụy is in his own element. Maybe Thụy will even become Vĩnh's guide. Thụy will pull him off the bus and lead him right into the guard room of Tang Frères supermarket. After reading the recommendation letter from Chợ Lớn, the on-call guard will happily take the two of them to see the director. After reading the recommendation letter from Chợ Lớn, the director will happily take the two of them on a tour of the grandiose supermarket. Vĩnh will take this opportunity to express his immense admiration for the director, having twice watched a French TV documentary on him, because without Tang Frères I would have nowhere to buy pigeons and vegetables to marinate in húng lìu and roast and make soup for him. He will suggest the director open another supermarket in Belleville to save me from the sixty-minute-each-way bus trip, which on Sundays only runs every thirty minutes, meaning I spend as much time on the round trip as on my daily commute to school. He will also recommend the director run for mayor of the 13th arrondissement and then for MP, so he can integrate Belleville into Chinatown and the

Chinese-French community will have a recognized political leader. The director will be so moved he will disclose to the two of them insider knowledge about Tang Frères and his own most classified leadership experiences. After the meeting is up, the director will take them on a citywide tour of the Tang Frères branches, warehouses, production facilities and outlets, and recommend they take the time to visit a Tang Frères restaurant to check the quality of roast pigeons and of duck skins stuffed with papaya salad, which he plans to serve President and Mrs. Chirac next year. Each with a notebook in their hands, Thụy and Vĩnh will jot down as they go everything they hear and see, complete with diagrams and illustrations. Back home that evening, the two of them will compare notes and type up a summary of the most important points. Vĩnh will surely remind Thụy to make two copies of the file with two different names, and save these on two floppy disks to hide in two different places, so they'll have a backup if the international mafia gets hold of one. Their plan for the next thirteen days consists of visiting the thirteen most celebrated companies in Chinatown. After reading the recommendation letter from Chợ Lớn, each on-call guard will happily take them to the director. After reading the recommendation letter from Chợ Lớn, each of the thirteen directors will happily take them on a tour of their respective company. Vĩnh will take the opportunity to tell them how he has seen their names and likenesses in Roast Duck magazine. He will also say that without the services of their thirteen companies, ethnically Chinese people in France would have nowhere to cut their hair, buy their clothes, shoes, bags, suitcases, and belts, nowhere to find their husband or wife, and then nowhere to order their wedding dresses, wedding cakes, wedding banquets and bridal makeup, and after that nowhere to rent a one-bedroom apartment where they can live and plant vegetables and raise children or make ties. Vĩnh will suggest they open thirteen branches in Belleville to save me from the sixty-minute bus trip to tour Olympiades and the climb to the eighteenth floor to have my hair cut and styled by Mlle. Feng Xiao. The thirteen directors will be so moved, they will disclose top secret insider knowledge from each of their thirteen companies and their thirteen sets of leadership experience. Thụy and Vĩnh, each with a notebook in their hands, will jot down as they go everything they hear and see, complete with diagrams and illustrations. Back home that evening, the two of them will again compare notes and type up a summary of the most important points. Vĩnh will again remind Thụy to make two copies of the file with two different names, and save these on two floppy disks to hide in two different places, so they'll have a backup if the economy police steal one of them. Thụy will spend his last two days in France composing an ultradetailed report, each detail illustrated by an even more detailed diagram. Three hours before departing for the airport, he will divide the twenty-eight floppy disks and two twenty-eight-page reports into two identical piles, wrap them in antimoisture wrap, then add another special plastic wrap, then put them into two leather briefcases with combination locks, then write down the combinations in two notebooks, and finally put one into the right pocket of his boxers and the other into the left, à la Vĩnh's anti-Parisian pickpocket measure. When all is said and done, he will tell Vĩnh that the last two weeks have been so hectic, he just never had the time to go see me. We haven't been able to meet for a meal or a stroll in Belleville park, but we should at least spend some ten minutes together before he leaves. Vĩnh will hem and haw. There has never been any family portrait in his mind. He will feel embarrassed, for himself, and then for me and Thụy. He will say nothing. He will ponder. He will continue to feel embarrassed. He will be about to ask if Thụy is sure that it's a good idea when Hao Peng and his father come to say goodbye and to leave a package for two fellow Hangzhouese who are now contractors in Chợ Lớn, a pair of ties and two aluminum

Eiffel Towers bought in Tati and imported from Asia just last month. Thụy will show them his report. They will nod at every line. Vĩnh will make a phone call. In less than two minutes the room service lady will appear at their door with four servings of roast pigeons, four duck skins, two cans of Tsingtao, and two bottles of Coca-Cola. Thụy will ask her to please go get some ice from the refrigerator when Hao Peng suddenly asks why the report makes no mention of Chinarama. His startled father will ask, so you two really haven't been to Chinarama. Thụy will reply, what's Chinarama. Vĩnh will repeat, what's Chinarama. Hao Peng and his father will both look at their wristwatches in panic, then bundle Thụy and Vĩnh into a lime green BMW. It's only fifteen kilometers from Belleville to the commune of Maisons-Alfort, but Sunday afternoon traffic clogs the way. Two rows of fitfully honking cars are stalling in front of The East Is Red, the owners getting out at times to greet one another, hey have you gone stir-crazy yet. Hao Peng's dad will honk once and get out once to pay his dues, then wait another five minutes before taking a forty-five-degree turn to glide into the taxi-only lane. Out of nowhere another twenty lime green BMWs will dash after him. The traffic police officer hasn't even had time to blow his whistle when the twenty-one BMWs pass the red light at sixty kilometers per hour, a rolling rice field to the tune of The East is red we have Mao Ze Dong. With Hao Peng's dad still driving in the vanguard, Vĩnh will raise his voice and sing, the East is red, the sun is rising, we in China have Mao Ze Dong, he is the people's savior, tra la la la, our people are happy in our abundant peace. Thụy and Hao Peng will clap the rhythm. The twenty BMWs still patiently trailing behind them, the twenty boys inside will raise their voices together with Vĩnh in a chorus, the forty adults will clap the rhythm together with Thụy and Hao Peng. Three minutes later the rolling rice field will roll past the Place de la Bastille, where eight rows of cars are honking and owners are getting out to greet one another, hey have you gone stir-crazy yet. Three minutes later again the rolling rice field will roll past the banks of the Seine, where a fleet of cruise ships are also endlessly rolling, as it turns out after a short while, to the tune of The East is red we have Mao Ze Dong. Vĩnh now raises his voice for the fifteenth time, the East is red, the sun is rising, we in China have Mao Ze Dong, he is the people's savior, tra la la la, our people are happy in our abundant peace. The rice field stops rolling and Thụy and Vĩnh can now see an arch made of concrete, crowned with "Chinarama" in the Latin alphabet flanked by the two heads of a two-headed snake, also made of concrete. Hao Peng and his dad, one on each side, will pull Thụy and Vĩnh out of the car. Turns out beyond the arch there are thirteen concrete pagodas made from the same mold, connected by a single winding concrete road whose shape the human eye can't discern but which the media insists a satellite can see says "Chinarama" in Chinese characters. Hao Peng and his dad will lead the way. Hao Peng's dad will explain along the way that on Sundays the director of Chinarama sees no one, on Sundays Chinarama hosts twenty weddings, twenty birthday parties, twenty first-year birthday feasts, twenty round-year birthday celebrations for the elders. Hao Peng will add, on Sundays Chinarama welcomes two hundred grandpas to practice twenty ways of breathing, two hundred grandmas to practice twenty ways of drawing butterflies dancing amid flowers, two hundred schoolboys to practice twenty sword moves, two hundred schoolgirls to practice twenty ways of shaping har gow. Passing beneath the concrete arch with the two-headed snake, Hao Peng and his father will surely scrutinize the map of the place. They will shake their heads at every page. Turns out what a satellite can see is even more confusing than what the human eye can. They will both look at their wristwatches in panic, then both pull Thụy and Vĩnh toward the nearest pagoda, the door of which reads "13" only when you get very close. A timorous crowd is already forming around the door. Two muscly young men, their voices ice-cold, will demand from anyone who approaches, your gifts, all of them. The visitors of 2004 won't have been able to find any aluminum pot, aluminum pan, aluminum basin, aluminum tray to wrap in red cellophane for a hefty offering, so each will wear a look of embarrassment as they produce a smallish sealed envelope from their pocket. Snip go the scissors in the hands of the wordless muscly men, and a single euro note will fall from each envelope. They must have found some postmodern artist to design the note, which after two years still startles the European common-wealth citizens who handle it, still makes them look twice. The muscly young men will hold each note up against the light, turn it this way and that, and smooth it out three times before putting it in a translucent plastic box, looking up at the visitor and asking their name, and handing them a plastic flower the size of a rice bowl. The visitor will breathe a sigh of relief, receive the flower with reverent hands, open the safety pin, and pin it onto their chest. Thụy will try several times to elbow his way to the front and present the recommendation letter from Chợ Lớn, but the muscly young men will just shake their heads and wave him away. Hao Peng's dad will introduce himself as the director of the Paris-Hangzhou leather shoes store, but the two muscly young men will just repeat that on Sundays Chinarama receives no one on private business, on Sundays Chinarama welcomes two hundred grand-pas to practice twenty ways of breathing, two hundred grandmas to practice twenty ways of drawing butterflies dancing amid flow-ers, two hundred schoolboys to practice twenty sword moves, two hundred schoolgirls to practice twenty ways of shaping har gow. Giving up, Hao Peng and his dad will hustle Thụy and Vĩnh to the next pagoda, where the neat "3" on the door so brightens their hearts that they run straight inside. Out of nowhere two new young men appear, no less muscly and their voices no less ice-cold, your gifts, all of them. Losing no time, Hao Peng and his dad will pull Thụy and Vĩnh right back out of it. After an hour hurrying along the single concrete road which traces out "Chinarama" in Chinese characters, the foursome will have feasted their eyes on all thirteen pagoda doors, the numbers arranged in some mysterious order that's impossible to detect even from the vantage point of a satellite. When five bell strikes from Notre-Dame come over on the breeze of the Seine, Hao Peng and his dad will again look at their wristwatches in panic, then pull Thụy and Vĩnh right back out beneath the concrete arch and into the lime green BMW. Two hours have passed but the two rows of cars in front of Chinarama are still going strong with the honking and the owners with the greeting, hey have you gone stir-crazy yet. Hao Peng's dad will take a gulp of Coca-Cola and then, without any warning, steer the car in a graceful arc into the taxi-only lane. Another twenty lime green BMWs, having been lying in wait somehow at the crossroads, will need only twenty seconds to materialize at their tail. The pack will tear past the police and the red lights, going first at sixty kilometers per hour, then eighty, then one hundred and twenty, a rice field at first rolling, then arrowing, then rocketing. Vĩnh will squeeze his eyes shut in order not to see the speedometer, whose red needle stays fixed at one hundred and eighty. Now he is in no mood to repeat the song The East is red we have Mao Ze Dong. And he has no energy left to turn back and see if the lime green field is moving to the tune of Michael Jackson or Madonna. He only allows his eyes to crack open when Hao Peng pulls him out of his seat. He lets them crack open a little more to see Hao Peng's dad pulling Thụy out of his seat. Vĩnh will need a whole bottle of Coca-Cola to recover from the ordeal. Panicked, he will then realize that all the other passengers are already lining up to board the plane. He will help Thụy fill out his customs declaration in French. He will tell Thụy to put his money away and not to attempt to pay fifteen dollars in airport fees. He will carry Thụy's two identical leather briefcases with their combination locks. When Thụy has presented his passport to the immigration police and is about to go into the waiting area, Vĩnh will run after Thụy to hand over the briefcases, and insist that Thụy call him as soon as he arrives back in Chợ Lớn. Thụy will promise to update him on the project of the hundred and thirty 13th arrondissements. Father and son will look at one another in silence. Thụy will urge him to excel in both school and Chinese classes. Vĩnh will tell Thụy to save his worries for the project, he himself already tops his class in math and English, and is only the teeniest bit behind Hao Peng at translation. He will tell Thụy about his plans to practice table tennis twice a week from now on, to parachute into Baghdad one day, and to build Belleville's very own website to facilitate its rapid integration into Chinatown. When the announcement comes over the loudspeaker that Thụy's plane will depart in fifteen minutes, father and son will exchange another silent look. Thụy will tell Vĩnh to go back, lest he keep Hao Peng and his dad waiting. Vĩnh will hesitate for a second, then ask if Thụy has anything to say to me. Thụy too will hesitate. He will hem and haw the same way the boy did three hours before. He doesn't know what to say to me. He was the one who said we should at least spend some five or ten minutes together before he leaves. But he doesn't know what he would say to me. In this regard, he is no different from me. He can't imagine us meeting again. Seventeen years ago, having returned to Hà Nội from Leningrad, I didn't know he still lived just a street away. By the end of summer in my third year, I'd lost all hope of ever seeing him again. Leningrad. It snowed even in May. My whole day was spent either in the classrooms, the library, or the autonomous territory that was my girlfriends' dorm-*cum*-nursery. June came, and time no longer existed. I buried myself in the ten subjects for the national exams. July came, the whole dormitory was in a purchasing frenzy for their overseas crates. My friends looked at me with concern. Your handful of items aren't worth the labor lost.

The hammering of nails, the transportation fees, the two immigration forms, the trips to send and receive. They discussed, they fussed. They disagreed. They quarreled. They told me, you decide it. The next day: you decide it. The next day again: you decide it. Finally: you just stand and watch. They packed, they stacked, but my handful of items couldn't be made any less pitiful, lying forlorn in the corner of the crate. They looked at me with concern. They waved a dismissive hand. They lined up to fill my crate with a TV set, a bicycle, an electric cooker, a toaster oven, an AC unit, a stroller, a set of aluminum chairs and table, a folding bed, a plethora of things I didn't know. How they sealed the crate, where they took it, how much tax they paid, what procedures they went through, I didn't know anything at all. They gave me a list. They said, when you're back in Hà Nội you take your time to stroll in the park with your architect sweetheart, we'll take your handful of items right to your block, carry them up to your floor, even hand them over to your parents. August the first, I boarded the train to Moskva. I was the first to leave the dorm. My friends were to linger till the end of summer, savoring every moment left. I got on the bus. I didn't know what to say. They looked at me with concern. They followed me onto the bus. Suddenly the bus was transformed into a traveling nursery. The driver asked, where are you merry girls heading to. They pointed at me and said, this girl here is going back home to get married tomorrow. The driver asked, so who's the lucky victim. My friends said, oooh, he's very handsome, very artistic. They knew nothing about my mother's letter. They carried on joking, the two of them are going to build a thatched hut on the bank of the Red River for their golden hearts. He's an architect, he can design the hut himself. The driver burst out laughing. The uncomprehending babies also laughed. The bus rocked with laughter. My smile was crooked. My friends were still joking breezily, are you having butterflies now that you are going back to him. You see his face at the airport, you punch it five punches, for the five years you wasted your youth waiting. I couldn't join in with their laughter. The driver, no less breezily, my fiancée couldn't wait five years, I left the army in April '45 and went back to my village, she already had two kids, the baby in her arms, the toddler standing by. She jumped on me and punched five punches in my face, then broke down crying inconsolably, she cried for five days straight. I was terrified, her husband was terrified. Even her two sons were terrified. Their cries deafened the village. The whole village came to see what was happening. On the sixth day she stopped crying and fell asleep, and I tiptoed out. I've been driving this bus ever since. My friends teased him, so how long was it before grandpa found a new grandma. The driver grinned, after five years I also got two sons. And each of them has had two sons of their own. When the bus arrived at the station, the driver shook my hand, send my regards to your architect. You punch him five punches in his face for me. My friends chimed in, and remember to cry for five days and nights straight. I burst out crying. The laughter stopped abruptly. They looked at one another in confusion. The uncomprehending babies also cried. The bus was in chaos. My friends were confused. The driver was confused. Passersby glanced up at us. It was August, and people were packed into the station like sardines. Roses. Fountains. Flags with the hammer and sickle. I wiped my tears. I got off the bus. My suitcase, the same one I brought from home five years ago, was carried by the boys onto the train, and placed right by my seat; at some point the girls thrust in a plastic bag, and when my parents opened it all in Hà Nội two days later, the chocolate inside had made a lumpy mess on the postcards and handkerchiefs. I remember none of what came next. And I remember nothing about going to the airport. A classmate from the language school in Thanh Xuân University came to pick me up when the train arrived in Moskva, took me to her dorm, went out of her way to call a taxi for me the next day, and took me all the way to the departures waiting area. In thirty minutes she managed to get me into a new outfit, comb my hair in a neat parting, put some rouge on my cheeks and some red on my lips. She looked at me with concern. Seeing you like this, no one would imagine you are returning from the West. Seeing you like this, your parents will be disappointed, your neighbors will be disappointed, we who are your friends will be ashamed. She shoved the lipstick into my hand. She thought for a while and then stood up. She dashed across the waiting area and somehow got hold of another classmate from Thanh Xuân. They must have concocted a plan between them, because twelve hours later when the air hostess announced that the plane was about to enter Vietnamese airspace, the new girl set on me with zeal, recombed my hair and repainted my lips, straightened my new outfit and shook her head, seeing you like this, no one would imagine you are returning from the West. On the plane they served us three meals, and she bullied me into eating. She picked at a few lettuce leaves from her tray and pushed the rest of its contents onto mine. All I could manage was a hard-boiled egg and some segments of orange. She looked at me with pity, seeing you like this your parents will be disappointed, your neighbors will be disappointed, we who are your friends will be ashamed. The air hostess went by with her cart. The girl nagged her for another meal. The air hostess glared at her. The girl said, this girl here is anemic, either you feed her or you call a doctor. The air hostess shook her head, and produced three slices of bread and a piece of butter. Gleefully the girl handed them to me. I didn't touch any of it. Again she looked at me with pity, seeing you like this no one would imagine you are returning from the West. I had to pretend to sleep before she would leave me alone. At Tashkent the plane made a two-hour layover; new passengers piled in. My classmate was reunited with a friend who studied journalism. They took out a muskmelon as big as a vat and cut it into slices. The musky aroma invaded the plane. The other passengers turned their heads. The air hostess also came over, shook her head and went away. They chomped and champed gleefully. They gave me a slice. I didn't touch it. The journalist girl asked, why so blue, did your beau dump you. I didn't answer. She went on, you think you're blue, wait until you hear about me. I lined up for a whole day to buy a stroller, hadn't even packed it in a crate when I got the news that my beau had got married. He wrote to say he couldn't wait five years, when I'd been gone for exactly four years and six months he upped and married this girl next door whose fiancé had gone to Hungary as technical labor, supposedly for three years, then four years, but now five had passed and he was still MIA. I broke down crying inconsolably, I just wanted to throw it all away, the ten subjects in the national exams, the red diploma. I wanted to take the stroller to his place, throw it at his door, and punch him five punches in the face, for the five years I wasted my youth waiting. My mom warned me before I left for the USSR. She told me that five is a fateful number. Her first beau couldn't wait for five years either. He went to fight in the South, and took up with a young army guide at some point. He left the army and came back to the village with two sons, the baby in his arms, the toddler standing by. My mom jumped on him and punched him five punches in the face, then broke down crying inconsolably. The uncomprehending boys also cried; they deafened the village. The whole village came to see what was happening. On the sixth day the boys fell asleep, and my mom stopped crying and left the village. She warned me, but I didn't heed her warning. She also told me that if I wanted to defeat the fateful number five, I must come back in the fourth year and get engaged. I didn't listen to her. I didn't want to waste money on a plane ticket. I didn't even dare spend two rubles on a plastic tablecloth. I backed off from a fifty-kopeck ice cream, reasoning I could always have one in Hà Nội later. I avoided cafés and restaurants and jewelers. I skimped and saved and so bought thrice as many things as others could. Once my own room started running out of space, I asked for help storing the contents of my overseas crates all over the dorm. I don't know if I can cry for five days and nights the way my mother did. Now I have to finish this melon to have the energy to wait for my crates. When I get my stroller I'll take it to the bastard's, throw it at his door and punch him five punches in the face, for the five years I wasted my youth waiting. She turned her attention to the melon, which they finished in a few more chomps. The air hostess shook her head as she went by. They gleefully agreed to slice up another. All night long I dreamed that I jumped on Thụy and punched him five punches in the face, over and over. Somehow I ended up punching the journalist girl. She shrieked in laughter. She said, this girl doesn't know how to pack a punch. You need more milk and butter in your system. When you get home you get some padded gloves, you hang up a sack of rice, and you practice daily like the pro boxers do. When you're sure you can take him down with a single punch, that's when you go find the bastard. You throw a punch, you watch him fall, you yank him up, you land another. When he thrashes like a fish you hold him by the neck and swing a third without delay. If he bleeds all over his eyes nose and mouth you wipe it with your hankie and then you smash a fourth. The fifth is the knockout, you have to sock him square on the vomer. If he weeps and begs, you shout at him to be quiet and you aim right for the bridge. Don't forget to check your glasses before you go. Don't get cold feet. Don't wax sentimental. Five punches in rapid succession before you stop. Don't miss any; you'll have to count to make sure. You punch once and you count one, you punch twice and you count two. Count loudly. You count to egg yourself on. You count to intimidate your opponent. The bastard feels your counting no less than your punches. The journalist girl lectured on, punching the air as she spoke. My classmate gleefully clapped for her. Both asked to come with me, come help me teach the bastard a lesson. One would hold his arms and the other his legs, and I could punch my five punches of justice in his face, they wouldn't consider it done until his vomer was smashed up. They didn't trust me to handle it myself. They looked at me with concern. They picked out a few lettuce leaves for themselves and then shoved the rest of their meals into my tray. I didn't touch any of it. My own meal was still intact. They looked at me with concern. They sliced up another muskmelon, champed and chomped their way through half of it, then shared the other half around the rest of the passengers. The air hostess also got a slice, which she ate while shaking her head. My parents also shook their heads when they saw me at the airport. My father joked, turns out Soviet butter and milk was no better than Vietnamese sweet catjang soup and pot-steamed pig brains. My mother looked this way and that, scouring for some hovering boyfriend, whom I would then shyly call to join us, shyly introduce, shyly ask to come over for some sweet catjang soup on Sunday. My mother hoped that five years would have made me forget Thụy. My father joked again, the suitcase from Hàng Hòm the Trunk Street turned out to be quite a brute. My mother waited and waited but no one came and said hi so that she could ask, what do you study, do you also have a red diploma, are you going to go back there for a predoc, what kind of family do you come from, which ministry or university are you going to work at, remember to come over for some lemonade on Sunday. After half an hour at the airport joking and waiting around, my parents were deflated. My father told me to give him the Hàng Hòm suitcase to carry. My mother told me to come home and have some lemonade, she'd bought a dozen lemons to help me quench my thirst, she'd stopped with the catjang soup once I left, having had enough with unwrapping government-store candies. The whole apartment block spilled out to greet me. Everyone praised me for not changing a bit during those five years, from the Hàng Hòm suitcase to the Hà Nội Department Store faux-leather sandals, from my hairstyle to my glasses, from my complexion to my bearing, from my height to my weight, the only thing new about me being my outfit, which looked borrowed. My mother had to give each person a piece of the lumpy chocolate before they left me alone. My parents' apartment hadn't changed a bit in five years either. Still two separate beds. Two mats. Two pillows. Fresh off the plastic bag on top of the wardrobe, my pillow lay grinning beside my mother's. Hà Nội was scorching the day my plane touched down, but then it drizzled for half a year; I went across the city looking for a job and came back home to stay in bed crying. My parents feigned obliviousness. They didn't mention the letter. They said I must try my best to get into a ministry or university. The first Sunday after I returned I was sent to my uncle and aunt's. They looked even younger than I remembered. My aunt still furiously shooed any proffered bananas. In the '80s the Vietnam-Cuba hospital had to construct a bunk on top of every bed but still overflowed with terminally malnourished patients. Their panicking caretakers were never calm enough to be creative in their offerings; everyone brought a round bunch of bananas, and every weekend my aunt had to rent a cyclo to carry two sacks to Bắc Qua market for consignment at a fruit stand. My uncle was the same. He also furiously shooed any proffered ducks. In the '80s the Vietnamese didn't know where their next meal was coming from, so the state-factory fowls got inevitably slapped with the "substandard" label to go to certain receivers. Every weekend without fail my uncle's employees brought over twenty ducks too substandard for them to sell in good conscience. My aunt butchered and plucked them without seeing an end of it, she must summon a girl from her hometown to come and help her with the butchering and plucking and then lugging fifteen of them off for consignment at two duck-porridge inns at the end of the street. My twin cousins, now two kid giants, still screamed bloody murder at the smell of duck, whether fried or roasted, boiled or braised with lotus seeds. The girl from my aunt's hometown also screamed bloody murder. She said she too was afraid of a surplus of duck fat in her blood. She ate only fruit, to benefit her complexion. The first time I came over, she was half lying, half sitting on the sofa, honeydew in her mouth, slices of cucumber on her face, listening to Khánh Ly while painting her nails, each foot submerged in a big bowl of water. Having done with her nails, she drew up her feet, she cleansed and she rinsed, she rubbed and she scrubbed, she whipped out tiny scissors and a tiny file, she trimmed and she filed her ten toenails, she rubbed and she scrubbed some more, she wadded her toes with cotton wool, she took out a blood-red bottle and painted her ten toenails, then took a ginger-yellow bottle and painted an apple the size of a toothpick end in the middle of each nail, then took an ink-green bottle and painted ten leaves half the size of the apples, then took a sparkling bottle and sprinkled a particle of glitter, tiny as a needle tip but refracting all the colors of the rainbow, in the center of each apple. After an hour she held up her feet in front of the whirring Soviet fan and asked me if her pedicure was one of a kind in Hà Nội. Not waiting for my answer, she asked if her pedicure would be one of a kind in the whole USSR. Then, without losing a second, she proceeded to bare her heart to me. She said she trusted me, so she was letting me know that she was only going to butcher and pluck ducks a little longer before running off. She said she didn't have to pay for her food here, she had no rent or bills whether electric or water or garbage, she didn't have to spend a single đồng, and at the end of the month she pocketed tens of thousands selling feathers from the eighty substandard ducks, at the end of the year she got a red envelope from my uncle and aunt and two other from the ladies of the duck-porridge inns. Last year she asked a hometown friend to buy her two one-mace gold rings. This friend was now cooking and washing dishes for a jeweler's family on Hàng Bạc the Silver Street. When she wasn't cooking and washing dishes, she'd picked up their skill of testing gold, and now she could glance at the kissing fire and tell if it was real gold or fake, 91 or 92 or 93 percent or pure. This friend advised her to try and pick up a trade if she could. She told me she was just a bumbling bumpkin, but she knew that butchering and plucking ducks is not a skill, consigning ducks or bananas not a trade. She was just a bumbling bumpkin, but she knew that not even a genius could learn a skill at my uncle and aunt's, and if she ran off without any trade, even with her few maces of gold, she would have to come crawling back after a few months. And crawling back would be hard; if she jealously guarded even her bumbling bumpkin's pride, as small as her two one-mace rings, then my uncle and aunt must guard their Hanoian pride, a dozen times larger than hers, as if it were their ancestors' tombs. Not to mention the weekly scores of ducks growing more substandard by the day if left un-butchered and unplucked. The minute she stepped out of the door they would bring in another girl from her hometown to make her regret it. There was no trade to pick up at my uncle and aunt's, but she could learn to live high on the hog. She was a fast learner, and in half a year had already passed my uncle and aunt in the high-living department. My uncle might have worn checked shirts from Czechoslovakia and tweed-and-wool pants, but un-derneath were government-issue boxers, the better kind reserved for high-ranking cadres but still a Đống Đa textile factory affair, the cloth thicker than military-grade, waistbands that slackened as soon as you touched them, seams as crooked as fishhooks. My aunt might have covered herself in satin, but her fingernails were always stained with banana, her toenails were black all year round, and every month one of these blackened nails would drop off. But not this girl, no sir. She might have worn pajamas all year round, but these pajamas were washed daily with perfumed soap, then ironed until the creases popped and sprinkled with cologne inside and out. Her panties, too, she got her friend to buy for her, 100 percent made in France, 100 percent cotton, the size of her palm, when they were hung out on the line my uncle and aunt didn't even notice them. My uncle and aunt assumed that my aunt's rustling satin panties with lace trimmings were the last word in international panties technology. My uncle and aunt saw the girl constantly painting her nails and chalked it up to the bumbling bumpkin's attempt to imitate city ways. She had it all planned out, she told me. Her friend once met a Việt Kiều lady who hadn't even known how to use a file when she left, but was now the proud owner of a nail shop in Canada. The lady after a visit at the Turtle Tower stopped by the jewelry shop to commission a set of ten rings in ten styles, one to wear on each finger. The anecdote left her aghast, she said, she'd never met anyone living such a high life, flaunting such swagger. She would run off the day she got ten one-mace rings. These ten one-mace rings were her personal five-year plan. Not as a high-liver thing, but as capital. She would run off the day her plan was accomplished. She had contacted a service who took people to work in Czechoslovakia. In Prague she wouldn't settle for a job in a checked cloth textile mill or a shoe factory, no sir, she would use her capital to open a nail shop. She said that if the Việt Kiều lady from Hà Nội did the nails of Canadians, she the bumbling bumpkin would be content with the nails of Czechoslovaks. In any case, the Czechoslovaks were the most high-living of all socialist peoples. You must know your enemy as well as yourself, she told me. That's the key to success, you know. Recently I got a letter from my parents, informing me that the girl did indeed make it to Prague, and did indeed open a nail shop there, but had to close it down after a mere few months, because for all their fame as high-living socialists, the Czechoslovaks in the early '90s still bought scissors and files and paints to do their own nails at home. But the girl, always a fast learner, found another service which took workers to Germany, and once she got to Dresden she lost no time saying goodbye to East Germany.

She'd had enough of socialism, she said. East Germany had been steeped in it for forty years, they couldn't just tear down a wall and proclaim themselves the land of capitalists and moneylenders. Even if she was to open a nail shop in East Germany, she would be looking at twenty years in the red, at least. She could not eat the loss for that long, she knew her enemy and she knew herself, she ran off to the West and spent five years working in someone else's nail shop before opening her own in the suburbs, and when the year 2000 rolled around she unveiled a new branch slap-bang next to Berlin's Headless Church. In 2004 she wrote to my aunt and invited her to Germany, all expenses paid, to discuss management of yet another branch about to be inaugurated on the other side of the church; she said my aunt's high-living Hanoian ways had earned her respect, which was why this honor was going to her and not to her own mother and aunts, whom she could buy tickets to Berlin for and lodge in her house for two weeks alright, but would never dream of living with them or entrusting any shops to them. My aunt called her on the phone, crying and thanking her. Having lived for thirty-five years as a citizen of Hà Nội, my aunt was more than polite enough to act as if nothing whatsoever had happened, as if there had never been that afternoon twenty years ago when she got home from work to find the girl lounging on the sofa, painting her nails and confiding in me about her five-year plan, which irked her so much she gave the girl three slaps in the face, scattering honeydew and cucumber all over the room. The sulky girl stormed into the kitchen. She didn't run to her bed and cry; she took out ten ducks to butcher. She filled a big pot with duck blood, then put on gloves to pluck them. From the living room I could hear her nails scratching against the feathers and skins of duck after duck. My aunt glanced toward the kitchen and shook her head. Such a bumpkin, she said, always making a fuss about trade this and skill that. A trade without a degree, a skill without a diploma, would only earn her a life of butchering and plucking. My aunt's great fear was that my twin cousins, already two kid giants, would never touch a diploma or climb to any degree. She said she looked upon me with such envy, looked upon my red diploma with such envy. My uncle and aunt knew from years of experience that when my twin cousins came of age, they wouldn't even be able to get bananas from patients or "substandard" ducks from companies without a university-issued diploma, bearing a stamp from the ministry of higher education and vocational training. As party committee secretaries, my uncle and aunt had utilized party-issued diplomas, stampless ones which had been sufficient back then to pull the wool over eyes but would likely fail in coming times, so they were asking me to tutor my twin cousins for the upcoming exams, since the kid giants couldn't spell a single word of Vietnamese, let alone Russian, and were equally clueless when it came to addition and subtraction, let alone multiplication and division and fractions and decimals. My uncle and aunt said I could rest assured, I needed only tutor the twins until the end of summer and they would ask some party committee secretary they knew to get me into a ministry or university. Seventy-two hours back in my homeland, I signed such a contract with my uncle and aunt. I went to the large bookshop on Tràng Tiền street and returned with two sets of ninth-grade textbooks. But on the first day, I realized that my cousins needed no textbooks; just as my aunt had told me, all they needed was simply to learn correct arithmetic and good spelling. On the second day I realized something else that I doubted my aunt even suspected: they detested books and abhorred school. On the third day they announced straight out that they were bored stiff with my lessons. My lessons were worse than useless. Arithmetic and spelling were worse than useless. They looked at me, frustrated. I was no better than their father's employees who every weekend furtively shoved twenty substandard ducks into their gate and then furtively jumped on their bikes to blast off. The twins had never seen their father give those employees a pat on the shoulder or so much as a thank you for their troubles. They only saw him furiously shoo them and yell in their faces, take your substandard ducks and bury them somewhere, douse them in gasoline and make a bonfire for all I care. They looked at me, frustrated. They said, red diplomas, green diplomas, it was all in their meddlesome parents' heads. All their parents did was dream up scenarios to fret about. They themselves knew perfectly well that even in their own grandchildren's time the party's diplomas would still trump the red or green. Their parents accepted bananas and substandard ducks, but when their own time came, they would never touch even one single physical gift, they would accept envelopes only, envelopes that would never need to be bagged and lugged to Bắc Qua market, to be butchered and plucked, to be munched roasted and fried and boiled and braised with lotus seeds day after day. Envelopes in hand, they would bid a final farewell to all duck dishes. During the last fifteen years they had carried sixty syringes' worth of duck fat in their blood. During the last fifteen years they might as well have been banished to duck island. Their parents assumed that their duck-fed bodies contained only tiny brains. But they had it all planned out, it was only a matter of time. In five years their school would have seen enough of their faces, and would ask the Ministry of Education to hand out to each a high school diploma. In another five years their parents would have seen enough of their faces, and would ask the two hundred party committee secretaries they knew to hand out to each a local-branch secretary diploma. In yet another five years their local branch would have seen enough of their faces, and would ask the party to hand out to each a party committee secretary diploma. It was only a matter of time. When their three five-year plans were accomplished, they would be the youngest party committee secretaries ever, with the most brilliant future awaiting. They said I could go on teaching them on a false hope if I wanted; my contract with their parents was only oral, and even if I were to type it up with a typewriter it would never be fulfilled. No summer had gone by without their parents digging up some red or green diploma to come and teach them. The red or green diploma would disappear when summer ended, leaving two piles of textbooks and all the arithmetic and spelling unable to get in even if their heads were split in two with an axe. I'd better wise up and look for a job on my own, that was their advice. I was their cousin so they were giving me a heads-up out of pity, no red diploma had even been found a job by their parents. The party committee secretaries their parents knew never took in any red diplomas. Their parents didn't take in red diplomas either. I'd better hide my red diploma as best I could before coming to the door of any office. My twin cousins never tired of preaching at me. Every day I came to teach them they gave me some advice out of pity. Every day I wrote on the blackboard the four arithmetic operations and a text to copy down. They looked at me, frustrated. They didn't protest, neither did they threaten to report me to the vice-headmaster and headmaster the way my teenage pupils in the Parisian banlieues do now. They didn't hoot or toot. They didn't yawn or discuss steamy movies. They didn't know about steamy movies yet. On Vietnamese television in the '80s there was hardly any kissing on the lips, let alone a bed scene, so they couldn't shriek with laughter and gesture wildly with their arms and legs. They only looked at me, frustrated. At moments when familial piety ran strong they would shower me with advice, and when the advice ran dry they again confided in me their triple five-year plans. Thus the thirty-nine-degree August mornings went by. The two notebooks and pens I laid out on the desk stayed untouched. The blackboard I filled stayed unwiped. I suspected that my uncle and aunt saw everything and were simply feigning obliviousness. And I did the same. Lessons done, goodbyes said, I was back to wandering the city looking for a job. At first I only asked at places where my English degree might be of some use. Two weeks later, I knocked on all doors, metallurgy, water resources, geology, geography, even the food industry. At first I always left a xeroxed copy of my university diploma. Two weeks later, per the twins' advice, I hid my diploma and left only my CV. When August came to an end, on another thirty-nine-degree day, I went to my uncle and aunt's for the last time. They acted as if nothing whatsoever had happened, no contract between us had ever been made. My uncle was away, paying a visit to the new party committee secretary at the twins' school. My aunt was left at home to groan about what kind of school changed their party committee secretaries like a girl changes her clothes. I said goodbye but she didn't notice, and the twins were too apathetic to care. They looked at me, frustrated. They thought me an obstinate mule. The hired girl paused her plucking and ran out of the kitchen to whisper to me that when her plan was done and she ran off, she would surely let me know. When I took my bicycle to the gate, she ran after me to say that if her five-year plan was accomplished ahead of time and she ran off, she would also let me know. I got on my bicycle, not knowing where to go. In the last three weeks I'd gone to almost all the ministries and universities in Hà Nội. I didn't remember which places I'd left a copy of my diploma and which ones I'd left only a CV. I didn't know if I should return to those places and bulk up my dossier with further documents, asking them to please not forget me, I was ready to take on anything they had, if my English and Russian weren't enough I was ready to learn accounting, finance, secretarial skills, typing, my parents were ready to support me for a few more years of adult classes to get me into a ministry or university. That last day of August, another thirty-nine-degree day, I got on my bicycle, not knowing where to go. Seventeen years ago on that last day of August, I didn't know which was sadder, more bereft of meaning, Leningrad or Hà Nội. I didn't dare pass by Thụy's home, I didn't dare go near my high school. I didn't dare visit my old teachers or classmates. I avoided anything to do with Thụy. The flamboyant tree heavy with blooms. The stationer where we used to shop. The lamppost with its broken neck. The three-way junction where a madwoman was always trilling a verse learned from who knows where: from your side over onto mine, the sperm go to the front in a line, as endless as the thread of love, linking East Trường Sơn and West Trường Sơn. That junction lay right on the road home from school. The girls crossed it with their chins on their chests, the boys gave it a wide berth every time. Several times the traffic police brought out their handcuffs and hauled her to the station for distorting the lyrics and obstructing traffic. Several times the mental hospital in Trâu Quỳ brought out their ropes and hauled her into their van for assaulting medical workers and inflicting grievous bodily harm. A lone tree stump was left in the junction. Boys and girls could make eyes at one another to their hearts' content. A couple may or may not have been made, but the very next day the mad woman was back at her spot, trilling East Trường Sơn, West Trường Sơn. I was always the first to cross that junction. My classmates would holler after me, always the same thing, are you in such a hurry to return to your homework. Thụy was always the last. I didn't know what he did back there, I only knew that he was always the last. And no classmate ever bothered to ask him anything. My parents taking me home from the airport also crossed that junction; in the thirty-nine-degree one p.m. heat there was not a soul in the street save for the madwoman, still trilling her East Trường Sơn, West Trường Sơn. It was summer, no sixteen-year-old boy or girl was crossing that junction, no one made an excuse about taking out the trash or going to a study group at seven p.m. and then vanished among the dozens of couples taking refuge in the shadow of the trees. The guard who once composed three-page daily reports about Thụy gave me the most headaches. He was now retired and a new guard was occupying his room at school. In appreciation of his fifteen years of effective cooperation, the district police recommended the ward people's committee grant him an apartment, fifteen square meters, right by the gate of my parents' block. The residents still recounted how on the first day he brought a certificate of achievement, on the second day a soldier's backpack, on the third day a wooden trunk, and on the last day he led a delegation consisting of his wife, his younger sister, his younger brother, and a litter of children, who as soon as they passed the gate did a tour of all five floors. The next day his household declared that they would look after the bicycles for the whole block. He would be the secretary and the rest of the household the members of his party cell. He remembered the hundreds of bicycles by heart. No need to chalk on numbers or hand over parking tickets, no need to hear the children's reports or the women's reminders, he knew which bicycle belonged to whom, and at what time it was deposited or retrieved. No need to step out of his fifteen-square-meter apartment, he knew everybody in the block by name and by sight and by detailed life story. He would stop me as I went by and reminisce about the high school, when my class was the best behaved in the whole age group. He remembered the tiniest details. He could relate the most obscure anecdotes as if they had happened yesterday. He chattered on about how every year I was called up to accept the award, a box of chalks and two "Deer" notebooks, every week I was the one who raised the national flag for all the hatless students to salute. And he didn't forget about the Beijing goon, such a surly face, always standing at the back of the class. Spotting him from afar, I would act as if I was in a big hurry. But he didn't let me off. He waved. He called. He made a happy clamor the whole block could hear. Once when I cycled by his closed door there was such a complete silence I was heartened. Too soon; he sprang out from nowhere, and getting an iron grip on my bicycle handles he insisted that I leave my bike there and go in for a cup of tea with auntie and the little ones. None of his children had any aptitude for learning, he lamented. He boasted to all bike parkers how closely attached he had been to the same high school that gave me wings to fly to the city bearing the name of the illustrious Lenin. He declared that I was the only one in the whole apartment block who had ever set foot into the cradle of the international proletarian revolution, so he had every right to be proud. I finally found a way to go home without passing by his apartment, but it involved climbing a wall between the block and the grocery next door. After an incident in which both biker and bike fell into their gigantic vat of pickle juice, I took a pickaxe and spent three evenings carving a hole just wide enough to let the wheel through. That hole was my saving grace until the day I moved to the Đê La Thành blocks with Thụy. Once, three months pregnant with Vĩnh, I came back to see my parents and could not but shuffle my way past the guard's home. The two oldies must have had a pair of binoculars glued to their faces the way they jumped out when my bicycle was still far from the gate; they waved, they called, they greeted, they made a happy clamor the whole block could hear. They made me a cup of tea steeped who knows how many times and put to me exactly ten questions. So now you are in the Đê La Thành blocks, so third floor, so eighteen square meters, so papa doesn't need to go over there and carry your bicycle upstairs anymore, so your office is on Lý Thường Kiệt street, so you can now buy market vegetables with your salary, so you got voted a hero of the labor force of the year, so your workplace gave you a box of candied winter melon and two packets of dried pig skin for Tết, so they took you to Đồ Sơn beach for the summer holiday, so you swam for three days but had to take thirty packets of instant noodles with you. I didn't need to answer those ten questions, only to nod or shake my head. And the oldies only needed a nod or a shake to go, oooh, so this or that person's tale turns out to be so true, to be so wrong, to be so trustworthy, to be so untrustworthy. Not a single one of those ten questions was about Thụy. The two oldies acted as if they had never heard of any Thụy. They had kept bicycles for the apartment blocks for so long they had turned into Hanoians already. They were soft-spoken and mild-mannered, they padded each utterance with thank yous and sorrys, they greeted all bike-parking guests at the door, they ran after guests to bid further farewell, they even sent their regards to the guests' whole families. They now automatically cracked a smile every two sentences. And they were determined to acquire the final mark of the bona fide Hanoian, the ability to act as if nothing whatsoever had happened. They were determined never to mention the Beijing goon, whom the guard once caught nodding off during a military anniversary while the visiting colonel was reciting how Chinese gunners fired five cannonballs over the border and our soldiers and people of the town of Đồng Đăng fired five Soviet mortar shells back. I also acted as if nothing whatsoever had happened. I also acted as if the two of them had never met Thụy. My own display of this very Hanoian ability didn't surprise me. Six months after getting married, I was prepared for any situation that might be thrown at me; I knew what to do when somebody solicitously asked me again and again, has your husband found a job, how many tables and stools did he make you, so you two live on a single set of ration stamps, is a single income enough for housing and electric and water and garbage bills, how are you able to buy market vegetables, who uses your quarterly tube of toothpaste and who goes without, how will you manage when you have a child. I ignored it all. I changed the subject. I acted as if I didn't hear. I gave a nonanswer. I told a blatant lie. To any solicitous question, I gave a solicitous reply. Six months after getting married, I now knew how to make people bored, and knew enough to understand that when people are bored they leave me alone. Six months after getting married, I had already given Thụy numerous chances to witness my very Hanoian ability. At the wedding, he witnessed how with a straight face I changed the subject, and with a straight face I told my friends that he was between offices. Twelve hours later, he witnessed how I nonchalantly declared to the apartment block that he was charged with a most important, most urgent project, on which he had to work at home day and night. A week later, he witnessed how with a light-hearted smile I said to the lady next door that we were such picky eaters we only finished half of our monthly twenty-four kilograms of government-store rice, the other half was always sold back to the store to avoid cluttering our space, anyway we only bought it in order not to waste our ration stamps because my parents were always pestering us to stuff our refrigerator with meat and fish and lard and fish sauce from their own, what they feared most was that we being too lazy to cook would just eat out and come down with a bad case of the runs and they would have to come fussily over and nurse us back to health. A month later, he witnessed how I solicitously replied to the question of the head of the local civil unit that his parents were both high-ranking cadres whom the party and government had recommended to stay and enjoy a special-track retirement in Vietnam, his younger siblings were all settled with jobs even more prestigious than his, each charged with several most important, most urgent projects, on which they had to work at home day and night. Six months after getting married, he'd had sixty chances to witness my very Hanoian ability. After a year living at the Đê La Thành blocks, I had become a bona fide citizen of the capital. But he didn't react. Maybe he was used to the very Hanoian ability of his mother, who for the past ten years had been solicitously replying to ten thousand questions of her old classmates, her ladies next door, the heads of her local civil unit. Maybe he knew that there was no other way. Or maybe he himself was acting as if nothing whatsoever had happened, maybe he also possessed the same very Hanoian ability. His name stayed ethnically Chinese and his birthplace stayed Yên Khê, but otherwise he had also turned into a bona fide citizen of the capital after twenty-eight years living there. I didn't know. Three hundred and sixty-five days after getting married, the only thing I cared to know was that he was still here. The eighteen-square-meter apartment in the Đê La Thành blocks. The double bed in the innermost corner. By its side the bookshelf he made for me. In the middle of the room, the small table with the couple of little stools, also made by him. He and I sat there for tea in the mornings. I read to him from books in the late afternoons. I told him about Leningrad. The white nights. The Neva. The moving bridges. The winters without him. In those three hundred and sixty-five days, I needed nothing else but him. In those three hundred and sixty-five days, I thought of nothing else but the moment he would leave. There was no Freud yet in the main library of Hà Nội but I didn't need Freud to tell me I was afraid of losing him. People are obsessed with what they fear. In those three hundred and sixty-five days, I only thought of the moment he would leave. In those three hundred and sixty-five days, I only waited for the day he would announce that he'd had it up to here with Hà Nội, he was going to board the train to Chợ Lớn. Ah, Chợ Lớn. Chợ Lớn, a name I hadn't even known. Chợ Lớn, the Hanoians said that in Sài Gòn there was a Chinese quarter as far from the center as it was dirty, the Saigonese themselves never set foot in it, the municipal people's committee gave them a cải lương opera house where no one ever saw a show, and a volleyball court where no one ever played a match. But Thụy said Chợ Lớn is the most important Chinatown in the whole of Asia. Ah, Chinatown. Chinatown, a word I had never heard before. Chinatown was never listed in either the English-Russian or the English-Vietnamese dictionaries. Chinatown was never mentioned by any English teacher, not in my three years of high school, in my five years of university, in the Socialist Republic of Vietnam or in the Union of Soviet Socialist Republics. Thụy left on the train, but my dismay stayed with me. Chợ Lớn. Chinatown. Why. Why. My Vietnamese couldn't tell me. My English couldn't tell me. At twenty-seven I thought Yên Khê was fate. At twenty-eight I thought Chinatown was fate. Was it normal or was it not. Yên Khê is the primal mystery. Chinatown is the final mystery. Was it normal or was it not. A year later in Paris, I had a friend with the name Yên Khê. Yên Khê told me that Yên Khê is such a simple name, as simple as mist over a brook. A year later in Paris, I went out of the door and people would ask me, is madame Âu going to China-town again. Yên Khê, Chinatown, still a mystery after ten years, still fate. Was it normal or was it not. A year later in Paris, my very Hanoian ability had no use anymore. No Parisian bothered to ask after Thụy, no one bothered to inquire after the boy's father; even if I told them my husband is a Chinese-Vietnamese, the Parisian would only shrug. Among those who shop at Tang Frères there must be a hundred thousand Chinese-Vietnamese, a hundred thousand Chinese-Laotian, a hundred thousand Chinese-Khmer, Chinese-Malay, Chinese-Indonesian, Chinese-Singaporean, so numerous the Parisian assumes the whole of Asia are ethnically Chinese, the whole of Asia speak Chinese, the whole of Asia have Beijing-style soup and Beijing-style roast duck for breakfast, lunch, and dinner. A year later in Paris, the white T-shirt lady on the Île de la Cité didn't care one bit about Thụy, who left a trace in the documents submitted to renew my permit only by his name and date of birth, and when I anxiously began to provide further information she waved a dismissive hand saying, don't ever dream about bringing the husband to France. A year later in Paris, I could pay my admission fee to the association of the capital's single mothers only to meet with some thousands of women raising children on their own. The thousands of women who upon meeting would ask each other how much welfare money they were eligible for, where to apply, what kind of documents were needed, whether insurance would cover psychiatrist bills for both mother and child, which lawyer to call if the child suddenly demanded to see their father, whether to tell the child to accept or decline if contacted by the notary and informed that the father had kicked the bucket and left a fortune behind, because declining would mean neither loss nor gain but accepting would risk inheriting a debt even more substantial than the fortune from the faceless dad. The thousands of women who would see one another and launch into a discussion about the relative merits of adoption, that the child would have a sibling in their life, that when we at eighty lie in an old people's home at least one of them will remember to come and take a peek, that when we at ninety lie six feet under at least one of them might bring us a pot of marigolds now and then. The thousands of women who would see one another and share the heartening news plastered all over the media that three associations of single dads were fighting among themselves for the nickname Roosters Raising Chicks and the right to partner with the association of the capital's single moms. A year later in Paris, I could introduce myself as a writer only to receive pitying looks and comments that if pen and paper saves me a visit to the shrink's couch, more power to me. Every September the book market would be flooded with five thousand debut novels out of nowhere, as soon as you stepped into FNAC you would be assaulted with a zillion authors and two zillion book titles, the reader feeling baffled would soon give up and come back home to their cozy stack of DVDs, where a mere hour and twenty minutes bestowed several Oscars' worth of entertainment. A year later in France, I could put a manuscript in an envelope and with bated breath send it off to some publishing house only to get a response months later, if I was lucky, that my manuscript had been read, had been found not so bad, but had not been judged to belong to any genre, whether thriller or romance or sci-fi, and therefore no one could figure out who would read it or in what circumstance. Ten years later in Paris, I've come to know that I was but one of twenty thousand writers of the same generation, living in the same city, embarking on the same search for a publisher, the same quest for our own unique voice, preferably a voice louder than the rest. Ten years later in Paris, I've come to know that other authors had great artistic traditions to back them up, whereas those from Vietnam, Laos, or Cambodia were only seen as representatives of the numerous wounds of war and poverty. Vĩnh says I'd better quit writing and take care of my silvering hair. In their most recent letter my parents implored me to finish defending my thesis and bring the guy home to do a round of the relatives. The guy himself never misses the chance, while running three laps around Belleville park, to dissuade me from antagonizing my friends and acquaintances. It's been a whole month since I added a word to *I'm Yellow*, not to mention a few short stories which are nothing but the titles, and some pages-long fragments that I don't know whether to call essays or what, whether to dispose of or keep. My ever-changing dreams are never the same length or setting, but all culminate with my sobbing and calling an ambulance, my ten fingers swollen into ten minibananas, infected by either a Vietnamese or Beijingese virus, struggling and fumbling to type a word, but the screen remains empty, gleaming green as cat's eyes. Last night I dreamed it three times in a row; spooked, I leaped up from my sofa and woke Vĩnh on his bed to tell him about it. What ridiculous dreams mom was having, he grumbled. I'd better find a husband and spare him the concern. At thirty-nine if I still run three laps around Belleville park every week, I can find a husband as easy as pie. Let him keep the black-and-white photograph. The piece of paper that my mother dictated and my father typed up and Thụy signed at the bottom should get chucked into the wastebasket. I should forget in order to live. It's the truth, forget in order to live. An hour later Vīnh leaped out of bed and woke me up on my sofa, blaming me for not only disrupting his sleep but infecting him with my ridiculous dreams. He dreamed that the two thousand Chinatowns were threatened with twenty million viruses capable of gutting them from the inside out, and after a week of intensive research twenty veteran computer technicians from China had found the cause but didn't dare make it publicly known, at least not yet. Beijing acted as if nothing whatsoever had happened, the Voice of Beijing never mentioned it, and the news was replaced with The East is red we have Mao Ze Dong playing on a loop. Rumors were quietly bubbling that the top computer expert of 2004, whose identity had been shrouded in mystery, had accepted from Beijing twenty million dollars and a tour of the Great Wall to engineer a male virus, four times as cagey as the bigender Y2K virus. Beijing had multiplied it into twenty million copies and slipped these into twenty million computers in two thousand Chinatowns all over the globe. All they wanted to do was understand the pace of economic development of Chinese diasporic communities. They couldn't foresee that those twenty million cagey male viruses could get out of the computers into real life and continue to gut our world from the inside out. Right now, Beijing was in negotiation with the top computer expert of 2004, promising another twenty million dollars and a tour around twenty forbidden cities to engineer a female virus of unprecedented beauty. Beijing would bring it home, take twenty-four hours to train it thoroughly in twenty-four stratagems of honey trap, then multiply it into twenty million copies to disperse among the two thousand Chinatowns. Vīnh said he dreamed that the whole world ceased their activities, even Iraqi guerrillas and American soldiers ceased firing at each other, to witness the historical encounter between the viral couple par excellence. Neither of us could get back to sleep. I sat down at my desk and managed another 350-word page of *I'm Yellow*. Vĩnh sat on his bed watching television. He promised to call for me if anything exciting came up. I stole outside as dawn drew near. It was cold even in May. In May 2004, Jacques Dutronc is still singing un milliard de chinois. Et moi. Et moi. Et moi. Everything was dark inside The East Is Red. I pushed the door open and went inside. The guard's snoring drove me back out. I made a round of Belleville market. Five trucks were being unloaded. The vegetable girl called after me, madame Âu goes to Chinatown so early today. I helped her carry a tray of tomatoes, a tray of cabbages, a tray of cucumbers. When we came to the tray of lettuces, I realized I was wearing flip-flops on my feet and pajamas under my black raincoat. I waved a dismissive hand. My forty-nine colleagues would never be in Belleville at this hour to explode in a collective fit of stress. They would never be in Belleville at any hour. Belleville is the first to be crossed out in their version of a Paris map. The schools in the 18th, 19th, 20th arrondissements are the first to be crossed out in their yearly application for a transfer. They say they would need twice the salary to even consider those problem schools. Twice the salary to cover housing at twice the price, croissants at twice the price, sandwiches at twice the price, to guard over a bunch of pupils with twice the problems. They say that with the banlieues' problem pupils, at least their parents still come to meet teachers in their nightwear, but with Parisian problem pupils, the school can call or write or ask for an intervention from local government all they like, all they get back is radio silence. My forty-nine colleagues are all wary of the 18th, 19th, 20th arrondissements. My forty-nine colleagues, who once a year go on a sightseeing trip to Paris, to saunter along the stone quays of the Seine or dance a conga through the Louvre or stand in a row posing for photos in front of the Sorbonne. My forty-nine colleagues, who on the first day of school exploded in their first collective fit of stress when I said I live in the heart of Belleville, which in turn is in the heart of the 18th, 19th, 20th arrondissements. I waved a dismissive hand. The light was now on inside The East Is Red. The reception desk was still empty. The guard was practicing Taijiquan in the innermost corner. He looked me up and down, his gaze landing on my flip-flops. I was just thinking how lucky it was that my pajamas couldn't be seen under the ten-euro black raincoat when he jerked his chin up, your documents, all of them. I said I was going up to my husband's room. My husband is called Thụy, a veteran architect in Chợ Lớn. Again the guard jerked his chin up, your documents, all of them. I said I teach secondary school in a suburb of Paris, I already submitted my certificate of employment to the Cité. Again the guard jerked his chin up, your documents, all of them, again he looked me up and down to my flip-flops. I said I was not one of the owners of those fifty Chinese passports currently detained in the Saint-Denis police station, dubbed by the media "the steamy breeze from the red East." Again the guard insisted, your documents, all of them. I smiled, bù shì zhōngguó rén. I suspected that his French was limited to that one sentence. I smiled again, bù shì zhōngguó rén. When I smiled for the third time, he reached for his phone. Out of nowhere two muscly young men appeared, each lifting me up by an underarm. I struggled and shouted, bù shì zhōngguó rén. My flip-flops scattered across the floor. The more I struggled, the harder those gigantic hands gripped my arms. Bù shì zhōngguó rén. I shouted myself hoarse. Fortunately the door was just a few steps away; my pain only lasted for three blinks of an eye, and in a moment I found myself under a bodhi tree twenty meters high, the highest in the bodhi row of Belleville. I got up and found my flip-flops, put them on, straightened my black raincoat, and looked up to see the hotel door already shut, the muscly young men already vanished and the guard already back to his Taijiquan.

It was cold even in May. Jacques Dutronc was still singing un milliard de chinois. Et moi. Et moi. Et moi. I made another round of the market. The five trucks had been replaced by ten vehicles half their size. The fruit lady called after me, madame Âu goes to Chinatown so early today. I helped her carry a tray of oranges, a tray of red apples, a tray of green apples. When we came to the tray of grapes, the color of a Đồng Khánh schoolgirl's dress, I discovered that she was wearing flip-flops identical to mine but two sizes bigger. I suspected that under her raincoat of a nondescript color she was wearing pajamas identical to mine but two sizes bigger. The thought of the pajamas sent me hurrying back to The East Is Red. The reception desk was still empty. Strains of The East is red we have Mao Ze Dong came from the bathroom; the guard was doing a solo performance while waiting for water to brush his teeth. I climbed to the third floor accompanied by the faint strains of the East is red, the sun is rising, we in China have Mao Ze Dong, he is the people's savior tra la la la our people are happy in our abundant peace. Four identical red doors caught my eye. I stopped in front of the first on the right. I was reaching for the knob when I heard rhythmic panting inside the room. I moved along, but had not even reached the next door when I could hear more distinct panting, no less rhythmic but twice as loud. I turned and ran. I passed the first door on the left and wondered if I should stop, but then panting no less super rhythmic and thrice as loud made me clap my hands over my ears and run for my life. I bolted into the fourth room. The lamp on the table illuminated a room so square, so stuffed, containing a double bed whose sheets were so snowy white that I immediately tore off my raincoat, slipped off my flip-flops, dropped onto the bed, rolled over three times on the so soft and thick mattress, and kicked the blanket to the ground. I kept the two fluffy pillows to dream a briefish dream while waiting for Thụy. He had just gone out for some cigarettes. The three packets of Thủ Đô from our wedding lasted him a month and a half; he smoked sparingly, one or two a day. By the following month, the lack of nicotine had left him restless. I took my three meters of rationed government-store silk and sold it at the market for enough money to buy him six more packets of cigarettes. Elated, he made me the little table, where I sat to read, every now and then glancing up at his back, half hidden in the snaking wisps of smoke, the pencil behind his ear. I had woken from my nap but he had not come back. We hadn't been able to meet for a meal or a stroll in Belleville park, but we should at least spend some five or ten minutes before he left. That was what he'd said, so I decided to wait. At thirty-nine I knew what waiting felt like. At thirty-nine I knew what defeat felt like. I lay on the bed, counting to thirty-nine. I counted to thirty-nine thirty-nine times. There was a chest of drawers by the bed and a wardrobe in the corner, but I didn't know which to open first, or what he might have left inside. Again I lay down and waited. He had just gone out for a cycle. A whole day making tables and stools had left him stir-crazy. When I came home from work at five thirty, he would be waiting at the gate of the block. I went upstairs to prepare the rice pot and vegetables. He took his bicycle to go wherever. One time he cycled all over the neighborhood of Giảng Võ, then all over Cầu Giấy. One time he went up the Red River levee to the Black Ferry port. One time he even crossed Long Biên bridge and reached the town of Yên Viên when it was already seven o'clock. One time he got a puncture around Chèm, flagged down a golden-hearted truck driver who took both him and his bicycle right to our apartment block, and steadfastly refused our invitation to come up to have a wash and some tea. One time he dropped by Hàng Bài street, where he met an old friend from the University of Architecture who was now collecting tickets for the August Cinema. The friend said as escaping goes it was quite unremarkable, but he could watch movies to his heart's content, all from the deluxe seat, all cream of the socialist cinematic arts. The friend recalled how back in Hà Sơn Bình they could wait for a whole year before two culture service cadres showed up with their projector. The whole village would then spread plastic sheets in the middle of the rice field to see the North Korean movie, comprised of one long scene of our Korean comrades hoisting the flag and charging, which the villagers sighed over, feeling like they would never know what those Soviet dramas, GDR spy movies, Bulgarian fantasies, Czechoslovakian sci-fis were all about. He said he'd watched *The Idiot* three times today and still adored it, the fourth screening would be on in fifteen minutes, he would let Thụy in through the back door. Thụy concurred. He quite liked Dostoyevsky but hadn't read *The Idiot*. At nine, when he had done admiring the most charming visage in Soviet cinema, he went to the parking lot to find his bicycle seat gone with the wind. His friend had to take him home on his own bicycle, Thụy keeping his across his lap and clinging on for dear life. That was the latest he ever got home. After a year living together, I had grown used to his coming home only when the vegetables were already done, the rice pot already turned a full circle, the novel in my hands already a few chapters in; he would walk in sweating all over, his bicycle either covered with mud or with its chain coming off, its tire punctured, its frame bent, its seat missing. I sat up. Turned out the chest by the bed had no drawers in it, only a pair of snow-white bath towels, which, when I shook them out, released a pair of palm-sized face towels, also snow-white. Turned out the wardrobe in the corner had no drawers either, only a pair of robes so long, so soft, and so snow-white, the likes of which I'd only seen worn by Hollywood stars who emerge from their bathroom and walk to their terrace, sipping coffee over the *New York Times*. Not a piece of paper torn from a notebook, not an odd coin, not an old tram ticket, not a broken pencil stub, not a crumpled page from a newspaper, not a spot of cigarette ash, not a chewing-gum wrapper, not a sleeping pill bitten in half, not a cotton bud, not an expired telephone card. Turned out The East Is Red is that kind of world-class hotel where a guest cannot leave for a cigarette or a few rounds on his bicycle without a housekeeper coming to deep-clean his room. Again I lay down and waited. At thirty-nine I knew what waiting felt like. At thirty-nine I knew what defeat felt like. The room was snow-white. I had already searched the chest of drawers and the wardrobe. I had waved my arms under the bed. I had flipped the mattress. I had felt each and every bed slat. I had taken the blanket out of its cover. I had even upended the wastebasket. The only thing that fell out was a snow-white garbage bag. I had explored every nook and cranny of the bathroom. I had turned on the shower. The freezing cold water had rained on the tiles. I had opened the two packets of shampoo and unwrapped the two tiny bath soaps. I had lifted the toilet seat, stuck the plastic brush into the bowl, swirled two times and flushed two times, just to see a raft of snow-white bubbles rising up at me. I didn't spare the two fluffy pillows either; I removed the cases and pressed my ten fingertips along every centimeter. I lay on the bed and waited. A fifteen-minute snow-white dream lying on a snow-white mattress. At thirty-nine I knew what waiting felt like. At thirty-nine I knew what defeat felt like. The reception desk was still empty. Coming from the kitchen were strains of The East is red we have Mao Ze Dong, the guard was doing a solo performance while waiting for water to make his tea. I went out of the door accompanied by the faint strains of The East is red, the sun is rising, we in China have Mao Ze Dong, he is the people's savior tra la la la our people are happy in our abundant peace. Vĩnh was waiting for me at the gate of the block. He grumbled, what frightful clothes mom is wearing where did you go. He took my hand and led me upstairs. In thirty minutes he managed to get me into a new outfit, comb my hair in a neat parting, put some rouge on my cheeks and some red on my lips. He looked at me with concern. He said seeing me like this no one would imagine I was his mother, seeing me like this his homeroom teacher would be disappointed, his headmaster would be disappointed, he himself wouldn't but he wouldn't be proud either. He reminded me that at all costs he must be present at the final match of the municipal youth's table tennis tournament at two p.m. today. He was to play against Hao Peng, the reigning champion. His headmaster had urged the whole school to come and cheer for him. His homeroom teacher had already prepared a speech for when he climbed onto the podium. Whether he gets gold or silver, he will team up with Hao Peng to organize a table tennis club to help Chinatown children compete in tournaments all over France. He is determined to start it today, the very day he turns twelve. Nine a.m. on Sunday, we got into the Métro, and Vĩnh fell asleep even before we sat down. His head on my shoulder. His hair is cropped like Thụy's hair. His eyes are slanted like Thụy's eyes. The other three passengers in the carriage growled. Will the train start again or not, at least let us know that much. Three hours a day on public transport is no way to live. I turned and said I also spend three hours a day on public transport. No one reacted. The abandoned bag is still waiting for the special forces to come and investigate. I'm still wondering if I should stay put, or leave and catch a bus. My watch reads twelve o'clock.

PARIS, MAY 2004